# FAERY SOVEREIGN

## THE FAERY CHRONICLES BOOK THREE

## LESLIE CLAIRE WALKER

sfp

# FAERY SOVEREIGN

**When ancient evil threatens the heart of all magic, Kevin joins the battle...**

Magic's secret heart hides in the depths of the Faery realm, protected for millennia by mystery and shadow. Until the most powerful enemy the realm has ever faced invades. And Kevin becomes the only one strong enough to lead the fight.

He must find a way to save the faery princess Silver and square off against assassins and friends-turned-rivals to reach magic's heart before the invader strikes. But winning the race isn't the only thing that matters.

The more magic Kevin uses, the more he risks destroying everything that makes him human. And the enemy? She's a Horseman of the Apocalypse...

Failure is not an option. Kevin will win—or die trying.

# ALSO BY LESLIE CLAIRE WALKER

**THE AWAKENED MAGIC SAGA**

THE SOUL FORGE

(The Complete Series)

Angel Hunts

Angel Rises

Angel Falls

Angel Strikes

Angel Roars

Angel Burns


THE FAERY CHRONICLES

(The Complete Series)

Faery Novice

Faery Prophet

Faery Sovereign


SHORT STORY COLLECTIONS

Ink & Blood

Ink & Stars

Ink & Sword

# CHAPTER 1

THE TWILIGHT felt charged, electric enough to raise the hairs on my arms. Doug fir and hemlock, their enormous trunks furred with moss, stretched higher than I could see. The crow that had been following me cawed on an overhead branch, taking off in a flutter of feathers and a shower of sap and needles. Its shadow flowed over me like dark water, then wheeled away to the north, leaving me alone in the Faery wood, the Forest of Dreams.

Forest of Nightmares was more like it.

My name is Kevin Landon. Once upon a time, I was a human living in the human world. By day, I went to school, studying my ass off and angling for a college scholarship to a school far, far away. By night, I served as a go-between among fae and humans. Magic allowed me to hear other people's thoughts when things got danger-ous. I didn't like it, because all I'd ever wanted to be was normal, but you couldn't wish away reality, could you?

If you'd asked my greatest fear, I'd have told you it was that I'd go too far over the edge into magic. Lose my humanity.

Then a girl I knew cast a spell that turned my city of Houston, Texas into a burnt-out shell of its former self. The office towers downtown looked like a bomb had gone off—steel frames bent and twisted, glass windows shattered all over the streets and sidewalks, concrete crumbled. Most of four-and-a-half-million people vanished without a trace. They were the lucky ones.

The ones who remained were transformed into the things that terrified them most, including me. White-feathered fae wings grew out of my back and my senses became super strong. My emotions turned up to an ear-splitting, mind-numbing, heartbreaking volume.

We'd averted an apocalypse, but we hadn't been able to return everything and everyone to what they'd been before the spell. My best friend Rude was supposed to be working on that, but we had no way to contact him, so no way to know how that was going.

That was two weeks ago. This was now.

Insects buzzed in the trees and low over the soil. Flies with bright blue wingtips, dragonflies as big as swallows, and other bugs I didn't recognize. Frogs croaked in a strange harmony that seemed more like speech than song. I felt sure they were talking about me.

I took the last sip from my steel water bottle, tilting the bottle vertical to suck down the last of the liquid. The flat-topped stone I sat on rocked as I shifted my weight. I imagined it felt the same as me, unstable and wondering what the hell I was doing there, disturbing its ordinary life. The dying embers of the fire in of me glowed like dragon's eyes. A few fat drops of rain fell, pelting my head and hands, and hissed when they struck the heat.

The mossy earth where I'd slept beside Simone had almost regained its spring and shape, as if we'd never been there at all. My brown leather pack rested beside hers—his and hers. Except we weren't exactly a couple. I didn't know what we were, and she wasn't here—a fact that was seriously freaking me out.

She'd gone to get water an hour ago, and she'd insisted on going alone. She had more experience in Faery than I did. She knew what she was doing, and she'd be all right. She didn't need me watching over her like she was some fragile thing. She'd said all of that, raising her voice with each word, as if she was trying to convince not just me, but herself.

She had a complicated history with humanity. She'd grown up

human, but she had a talent unlike anyone else's. Her voice mesmerized. She could make people whatever she wanted them to. The Faery King wanted her for his own, so he'd marked her. She slowly became fae.

No one could refuse her golden voice. They not only felt what she wanted them to feel, they acted on those feelings. She could read people, too. Just one sound was all it took for her to have a lock on their hopes, fears, and desires.

The spell that destroyed the city, giving life to everyone's fears, made her human again. Whether that change was permanent remained to be seen.

She didn't want me to treat her like she was fragile, but she was newly breakable in a realm of magic, and she should've returned from the river a half hour ago.

The rain hesitated, the clouds far overhead not yet ready to let go completely. Wind gusted from the west, pregnant with ozone. I took a deep breath. It didn't stop the sharp claws of panic digging into my gut.

There were worse things in Faery than the potential for hypothermia after a thunderstorm. There were worse things than death. There were... things.

No matter what Simone wanted, I shouldn't have let her go alone.

I slammed the water bottle into the earth, my frustration and improved strength digging the base two inches into the soil. Pushing to my feet, I said a quick prayer that the campsite would remain safe and undiscovered by anyone other than Simone and me. I was still new to the power that came with being fae, but I was getting good at camouflage.

I forced myself to take a deep breath. On the exhale, I imagined the space behind my heart opening and connecting the well of life force in the realm of Faery, the energy from which all life in Faery—and all the other worlds—was created. That connection was the heart of what I was now. No longer just myself, but part of something bigger.

From my first step along the route to the river, the firs and hemlocks read and understood my intention, where I needed to go.

They *moved* to guide me, literally. The forest blurred around me. The air vibrated so hard, I could almost see the molecules of magic it was made of. Then a clear path appeared between the trees, the loam along the way subtly lit.

My steps felt sure, stepping over fallen limbs and seeking roots—more sure than they'd ever been on the cracked concrete sidewalks back home. I picked up the pace, covering the distance as if I were running.

Simone didn't have the same help from the forest or the same connection with it. Chances were, I'd find her in a minute or two with nothing more than a twisted ankle. I was only freaking myself out, blowing the situation out of proportion. She'd be all right, but moving slowly, or resting somewhere inconspicuous. It wasn't like she could text or call. Magic didn't mix well with phones.

Instinct spoke, a still, small voice in the back of my mind.

*Hide.*

The muscles in my shoulders contracted on their own, pulling my wings tighter against my back as I ducked behind the wide trunk of a fir. A twig snapped, cracking the air like a gunshot. I held my breath as a drop of rain landed on the bridge of my nose and slid down slow, trickling off the tip.

Three heavy, stumbling footfalls crunched on fallen needles. Underneath that cacophony, a moan of pain rose in a familiar, mesmerizing voice.

A single word bloomed in my mind like a poisoned flower. *Knife.*

It was a thought. Simone's, not mine. She was in danger, and she was broadcasting in the hope that I'd hear. My heart climbed into my throat.

*They're close.*

Just those two words. Nothing about who or what had attacked her.

Instinct screamed that I shouldn't move an inch. Stay hidden or die.

Simone was in trouble.

I broke cover as she staggered out of the brush, a flash of peacock feather halter-top and leather pants. She tripped over her feet and fell face-first, unable to get her arms in front of her to break momentum. I lunged and caught her by the shoulders, tucked my hands under her arms, and dragged her behind the fir. Her toes grooved the soil, which would point the enemy straight at us.

The forest hushed, suddenly still and silent. The insects and frogs didn't so much as whisper. The wind held its breath. The rush of my blood inside my head pulsed and roared like an oncoming freight train.

I couldn't see Simone's face through the tangle of long purple and black hair, but I could smell the stink of fear that rolled off of her in waves and taste the coppery blood that dripped from scratches on her arms, along with the deeper, richer scent of blood from a more substantial wound. I pulled her to her knees, where she swayed before she caught her balance. Only then did I let go long enough to brush the hair from her face.

Her eyes were wide, her voice pitched low. "The girl. She followed me. She—shit!"

The fine hairs on the back of my neck rose like antennae a split-second before lightning pain exploded in my right shoulder.

The world turned gray and grainy, then color flooded in again. I spun and—whoosh—something cut the air where my head had been. I glimpsed a wiry arm. A blade arced into a silver blur.

I knocked it out of the air, the edge slicing open my forearm before it dropped. Simone grabbed the hilt, scrambling away.

The attacker shoved me off my feet with supernatural strength. I crashed into the fir's truck, sliding down like a ton of bricks, the impact stealing my breath. She was on me before I could roll, punching me twice before I could raise an arm to defend. Even then, I couldn't block everything she threw. There was magic in her blows. And deadly intent. Every blow felt like a killing strike.

I reached with one hand for anything I could use as a weapon, but found only leaves and needles and dirt. I stretched, fingertips brushing something smooth and cool and hard. A stone. It tipped toward me, but not enough to grab.

The girl's fist collided with my left temple. The force of the blow rocked me to the core. Nausea exploded in my gut. Consciousness felt light as a feather, ready to fly away.

I reached for the stone again, focusing with every ounce of will I had. It tipped into my palm. I gripped it tight and swung for the girl's head, connecting with a solid crack. She shook it off. I swung a second time, harder.

The rain of fists stopped. She blinked at me, sucking air.

I bucked her off of me, drawing in my legs and kicking her hard enough to send her flying onto her back. I rolled to a crouch, dizzy and sick, black fae blood streaming into my eyes as she pushed up onto her elbows.

Tangled waves of brown hair brushed her freckled shoulders. The tips of her ears were pointed, and the gauzy tops of wings stretched at disjointed angles behind her. If she were human, I'd peg her age at thirteen, but she wasn't human and never had been.

She stared at me as if I were prey, her skin so pale I could see the dark pulse of blood in the veins at her temples. She tried to rise, but her arms refused to hold her. Her eyes widened and her mouth opened in a round O. A heartbeat later, she collapsed on her side like a deflating balloon.

I waited for a fake-out—if this were a horror movie, she'd get up again when I least expected it. But she didn't move again, not even to breathe.

I pulled in a lungful of air, trying to understand what had just happened. Only one thing I was sure of: it should be me on the ground dead, not her.

The crackle of twigs and needles behind me had me wheeling meet the next danger, but there was only Simone on all fours, closing the small distance between us. She held the attacker's knife in one tight fist.

"Kevin, get away from her. If she's sick, she's contagious to fae."

I shook my head. "She's not like the others we've run into. She was so strong. Stronger than any fae ought to be."

I duck-walked the few feet to her side and pushed one shoulder to settle her on her back. Her sightless brown eyes looked like empty glass. I reached to close them.

At my touch, the darkness I'd seen in the veins at her temples brightened, the shine fading to a plain, empty white. Spiral markings of the same white rose to the surface of her skin.

I yanked my hand back. "Damn."

The same spell that made me fae and turned Simone human had infected the fae world like a virus. We knew it spread, but hadn't yet determined how. We knew it was fatal, but had no metric for how long it took to kill. It took away the will to live. It turned magic against the magician.

"Every other sick fae we've seen got those as soon as the disease took hold," I said. "The hell is going on here?"

"Kevin, back away, please."

"She punched me bloody. Pretty sure I've been exposed."

"Don't joke about this."

I held up both hands as a sign of truce. "How did she find you?"

"I saw her in the woods on the way to the water."

"Did she see you?"

"I didn't think so, but I was wrong, wasn't I? She was hunting me, Kev."

*Hunting.* I felt cold at the thought.

The girl's hand twitched. I jumped an inch off the ground, landing on my ass. "You see that?"

Simone nodded. "Look at her skin."

Vapor rose from the girl, and her skin began to dry and crack, thinning as we watched, as if it were made of old paper. The wind picked up, lifting tufts of the girl's hair and tearing them from her scalp as easy as plucking flowers from the ground, the breeze carrying away strands like dandelion fluff.

My own skin began to crawl.

The girl's body began to shrink, sinking in on itself as if the flesh and blood and bone that gave it mass were wasting away. For the space of a breath, the air stank of rotting meat, then the stench vanished. Her fingers began to curl, her arms to roll up like a carpet for whom no one had anymore use. Her feet and legs followed. It was like something out of a cartoon, except it was real and right in front of us and terrifying.

Bile fountained into my mouth. I swallowed hard to keep from throwing up.

Simone's face paled. "God."

My voice shook. "You ever seen anything like that?"

She shook her head. "The other sick fae—they didn't do this after they died. This is something else. Something different."

"Something to erase any trace of who she was or why she came here."

"Why do you say that?"

"I don't know." I hadn't been thinking anything like that before I opened my mouth. I started to speak again, but it took two tries before I could articulate what needed to come out. "Even after people die, it takes a while for their bodies to really shut down. The blood's not pumping and the nervous system's not jumping, but there's still a kind of fading life there. Someone who knew what they were doing could use that to get information, kind of like you can still get DNA from a dead person, only with magic. Am I making sense?"

She nodded. "You're saying that she, or whoever sent her, set up some kind of self-destruct mechanism in case she died."

"Yeah, that's what I'm saying."

"You sound like a crazy person, Kevin."

No way around it—she was right. "Yep."

Simone rose to her feet. "Up. Turn around. Let me look at your shoulder."

I stood. "What about the cut on your stomach?"

"It's nothing."

"It didn't smell like nothing."

She made a face. "Kevin, that's gross. Anyway, if I say it's fine, it's fine."

I wanted to push, but her tone slammed the door shut on any further questions.

"Your shoulder is also gross."

"Sorry. I don't feel anything. It's like I wasn't even stabbed."

I couldn't see her roll her eyes, but I felt it all the same. "Must be adrenaline."

"The fae have adrenaline?"

"It's not that, but it's like that. Your body creates a kind of magical patch that blunts the effects of losing your darkness."

"It keeps my blood on the inside."

"So to speak. I can't see it well enough. Off with the stupid shirt, Kevin."

The one I insisted on wearing even though I'd had to cut holes in the back for my wings. Without the cotton covering my skin, I felt unguarded, too open—naked.

When her fingertips brushed my skin, they seemed to burn. I couldn't tell whether that was because of my heightened fae sensation, or because of how I felt about Simone. I blew out a long breath to disguise the intensity of the sensation and hoped she wouldn't notice.

She seemed one-hundred percent focused on my shoulder wound. "It doesn't look that bad."

The words should've comforted, but they gave me a shiver instead. "What aren't you telling me?"

"I don't know. Something about it feels wrong."

"You can't tell what it is?"

"No. We should get out of here. Whoever sent that girl will know by now that she didn't kill you."

"You mean 'us.'"

"I'm not anything for an enemy to worry about, Kev."

That wasn't true at all. I shook my head. "You know things no human could know. You still have the power of your voice."

"It's not the same. I'm just human now," she said. "You're not only fae, you're special. The King was afraid of you. He ruined your life. He kidnapped your friends and family."

That was how I'd ended up acting as an intermediary between humans and fae in the first place. The magic had risen inside me without warning, transforming me from a bereaved nerd in search of a scholarship to the first faraway school that would take me to an outright freak accused of murder, thrust into the secret hidden beneath the surface of the normal world. Magic was real. The fae walked among us. They considered me a danger, turning my life upside down, all because the Faery King believed I would someday take him down.

"He never tried to kill me, Simone."

"Because he believes you're important to the Faery realm itself. He's an asshole, but he's not willing to risk an entire world."

I didn't want to talk about the finer points of the King's douchebaggery. I didn't care about his reasons except for how they affected me and the people I loved. "My point is, this isn't him sending an assassin after me."

Her eyes widened.

My heart stuttered in my chest. "What did I say?"

"Assassin."

I furrowed my brow. "I was being sarcastic about that, sort of."

She shook her head. "There's so much you don't know."

"I'm aware. So, tell me."

"Walk, and I'll tell you. We need to get back to camp as fast as possible. Then we need to get the hell out of Faery."

I took a step in the direction of camp. The air vibrated. The trees *moved* once again, ready to guide me where I wanted to go, safely and easily.

Simone shuddered. "Good thing this forest is friendly."

"Yeah. What about assassins?"

"Magical assassins."

"You're kidding."

"Wish I was. There's an entire order. They take in kids whose magic manifests when they're super young. They train them to use their power to kill."

"How young?"

"Anywhere between five and ten years old."

"Jesus." I couldn't even imagine what it would've been like for my magic to rise when I was that little, with no way to explain how I felt or how scared I was, with no way to understand it or to even find someone who could help me. "This order, it takes them from their families?"

"Sometimes. Sometimes their families kick them out or institutionalize them, and the order picks the up off the street or from the hospital. No one else is looking out for those kids. The law can't help them. The cops don't even know about magic—the real cops, not the ones the King sent after you. Magic is a secret, Kevin."

"Because we hide it. Because we're afraid of what other people would do if they found out."

"No, Kev. Because it protects itself. Normal people don't even see it. If by some chance they've got some innate magical talent or ability and catch a glimpse, they'll find a way to discount what they've seen or felt, or make up a story so that what happened makes sense in the normal world. These kids are at the order's mercy."

Every word she said felt horribly true. "The dead girl isn't human. She's definitely fae. She had a fae sickness."

"That she could've caught when she arrived in Faery."

It made sense—if the girl was really what Simone thought she was. "Does the order take fae kids?"

"The fae and the angels and demons guard their offspring more closely. The worlds they inhabit are magic to the core. The chance that the order could take one of their kids is slim, and the risk they'd take in terms of violence and payback is too great. But the order has been known to take human children and…change them."

Like I'd been changed. Like Simone had been changed. "Her strength. The force behind her punches."

Simone nodded. "I think the girl is from the order. The question is, who hired them to kill you?"

I could see the girl in my mind's eye, arriving in Faery through a portal, the sickness striking her like a fist to the chest, mucking up her magic, her thoughts, and her body. I could hear her breathing change, heart beating too fast, and feel how even the act of stalking our campsite set the muscles in her thighs quivering like gelatin. My mind filled with her thoughts.

*Neither the woman nor her target was as on-guard as we should be. Easy prey.*

*If she waited until nightfall, or until we slept, she could complete her mission and get back home, where her mentor could tell her in clear words what was suddenly wrong with her, where the Order could drive away the dread that settled in the pit of her belly. But then the woman had left camp, heading for the river, and that presented a perfect opportunity to take out the one person who stood in her way.*

*When the woman didn't return in time, the target would become distracted with worry. He'd forget his magic, make stupid decisions. He'd be easier to pick off. It was only a matter of time before—*

Simone's voice broke my concentration. "Kevin, what are you doing?"

I stared at her, a chill overtaking me.

"Your fae intuition again?"

Maybe. No. Yes. "At first, I saw her, and then I saw us through her eyes, as if I were thinking her thoughts. I could feel the sickness take hold. And..."

"And what?"

"She was expecting backup."

"If she doesn't report in, how long before the order sends someone after her?"

"I didn't get that far," I said. "We shouldn't go back to camp at all."

"I want our stuff."

"If her backup arrives while we're there, we might not get lucky again. We can get more stuff."

She threaded the blade through her belt. "I left something there that we can't replace."

"What kind of something?"

"Later, okay?"

She would tell me in her own good time or not at all. "Okay."

We walked for a few minutes in silence. I kept my physical ears peeled for sounds that shouldn't be there. The huff of someone else's breathing. The rustle of brush or branch between gusts of wind. I kept my psychic ears primed, too, imagining them like satellite dishes waiting to pick up any semblance of a stray thought that didn't belong to Simone or me.

I didn't hear a thing.

The campsite looked just like I'd left it. The embers had cooled. Only a wisp of smoke rose from the center of the ash.

Simone grabbed her pack and took a step away from me for privacy, peeling open the flap and sticking her face inside. Whatever she'd wanted to grab was in the pack, and she'd been worried that it would disappear, or that someone would take it.

"Everything's good?" I asked, picking up my own pack and shrugging into it.

Her shoulders climbed towards her ears. "Fine. Everything's exactly where it's supposed to be."

"Then why are you tensing up?"

She slowly lowered the bag, hanging on to it by her fingertips. She looked at me with unfocused eyes. "I don't feel right."

I took the bag from her, slipping my head and shoulder through the strap. She opened her mouth to argue, then snapped it shut. She splayed her fingers, raising her arms as if she were trying to grab the air around her for balance.

"Hold on to me," I said.

She gripped the waist of my jeans while I reached for the hem of her halter, dragging it up to lay eyes on the shallow cut to her belly.

She hadn't been playing off the damage. It looked exactly as she'd advertised—except for the faint shine of magic around the wound, as if someone had sprayed it with a red mist.

Her voice sounded small and faraway. "I feel like I'm going to pass out again."

A heartbeat later, her legs gave way.

I pulled her close, holding her weight with one arm as the hairs on the back of my neck sprang to attention.

Trouble was close again, whether it was a second assassin or something else. We had only a minute or two before it was on us. Fear spiked in my gut, clawing its way up and out, tightening every nerve to the breaking point. If I didn't do something—if I didn't do the right thing—things would get bloody.

I gathered the anxiety rising inside me and focused it like a laser, drawing my magic around it like a coiled serpent ready to strike. I loosed it through my free hand, drawing a portal to take us through. The stink of sulfur bloomed all around us as the doorway opened into the In-Between, the moisture in the air heating until it bubbled and burst.

My strength ebbed as the portal formed. Drawing the doorway shouldn't have drained me so quickly. I didn't have an endless reserve of fae magic, but I had enough. The brighter the portal grew, the weaker I felt.

I hitched Simone up and over my shoulder so I could run with her if it came to that. Stepping through the portal, I whispered a prayer that the realm between worlds would shelter us. That the predators chasing us here wouldn't be able to track us there.

*If I didn't find somewhere safe to go to ground, we might not make it through the night.*

That wasn't fear talking. It was fae instinct, which meant that it was true.

# CHAPTER 2

THE ROAD TO THE IN-BETWEEN burned with the heat of a thousand suns—the friction of worlds rubbing up against each other. The hairs on my arms curled, singed to the skin. Simone's mane streamed behind her, sparks dancing in the black and purple locks. The feathers in her halter lit from within and shone like jewels.

A heartbeat later, I stumbled through the far side of the portal, tripping over my feet, going down on an oil-slicked street. I turned my body as far as I could to absorb the impact, Simone landing on top of me in a heap of pointy bones. We lay on broken concrete laced with ribbons of asphalt that'd been used for repair but had instead spread and melted into the cracks.

The warm air suffocated, the rotten egg taste of it making me breathe in shallow gasps. The gloaming had taken hold, drawing out shadows and making it harder to see creatures that moved within them.

I listened carefully, reaching out with the tatters of my magic. Were any portals open nearby? Did I hear any thoughts that didn't belong to me? Was danger lurking around the corner?

My hackles stood at attention. We were being watched. By whom —or by what?

Frogs sang close by, a rhythmic undercurrent in the hush of the night that jammed my signals. The full moon hung low in the dark sky, looking bigger than any moon I'd ever seen. Old, twisted oaks lined the street, nothing behind them—not a blade of grass or a bush or a building. No animal moved over there. It took me a minute to understand that I was looking at the outskirts of the In-Between. We'd traveled to the edge.

That left limited places to run and fewer places to hide. I hadn't been aiming for this place. I'd tried to get us somewhere safe. Instead, I'd put us up against a wall. We were cornered.

Simone lifted her head slightly. "Put me down, Kev."

I rolled her off of me as gently as I could. "You all the way back?"

"Where'd I go?"

"You passed out."

She pushed to her feet. She seemed steady enough as her gaze darted here and there, taking in the situation. "Kevin, open another portal now. Get us out of here."

"Can't. My magic is drained."

She stared at me. "That's impossible. The fae have an unlimited supply."

"Not this fae."

"We need to figure this out."

Yes, we did—as soon as we found a place to hide.

The oaks cast shadows on the road, their branches becoming gnarled fingers. I caught a glimpse of ruffled black feathers from the corner of my eye. A crow. A new one, native to the In-Between? Or had the same one I'd seen in Faery? One crow was like any other, at least as far as they dealt with me. They all seemed to share the same razor-sharp mind.

It perched on a wavering branch, staring down at me. The hairs on the back of my neck stood taller.

The wind gusted, stinking of dead things. Dreams extinguished. Bones cracked and sucked empty of marrow. Fish washed up on the beach, rotting in the sun. I pushed to my feet, knees cracking, my wounded shoulder pierced with a cold ache that I felt inside my teeth.

Suddenly, my wound didn't feel like nothing. It felt like everything. The hell was going on?

*Don't panic,* I heard.

Not my thought, and not Simone's.

I listened harder. I didn't hear any other thoughts. No, I didn't hear any other *human* thoughts. There was only one other being in the immediate vicinity.

I met the crow's gaze and held it. It didn't glance away or light from the tree, only stared back at me.

Pushing life force through the soles of my feet, through the cracked and patched concrete and into the earth of the In-Between connected me to the land instantly. I took a deep breath and opened up the space behind my heart, calling up my connection to the well of life force in Faery. Even though I was no longer there, I could sink into that energy, connect to my true nature. With every breath, my heart opened a bit more, allowing me to catch the nuances of the crow's words, the metallic edge to every syllable, the other-than-human intelligence of them.

My ears heard a soft caw. Meaning bloomed in my mind.

*Kevin Landon.*

It knew my name. I turned my thoughts toward it. *Who are you?*

*Guardians,* it said, speaking not just of itself, but its fellow blackbirds.

*Guardians of what?*

*You.*

*Who sent you?*

*You did.*

I hadn't asked anyone to watch over me. What the crow said made no sense at all. But it wasn't lying, and I sensed no magic controlling it. *You here to look at me or tell me something?*

*You and the dying human are not alone.*

*The dying human?*

The crow shifted its gaze slightly to land on Simone.

Oh, God, no. I curled my hands into fists. *What's wrong with her?*

The crow sent me an image of the fae assassin's blade.

My mind ran through possibilities. A curse. Poison. Or simply that the wound wasn't as harmless as Simone insisted I believe.

*How do I help her?*

No answer.

God damn it. If I could get her out of here and back into the human world, I could find a healer for her. Or I could take her to friends who could stop whatever was happening until we could figure it out.

*I need a door out of here. Can you open one to the human realm?*

The crow shook its head.

*Can you lend me the magic to make one?*

It picked up one taloned foot and slammed it into the branch, shaking loose a leaf that arced gracefully to the ground. *Not safe here.*

Simone grabbed my arm. "Kevin, what is it?"

"A warning."

The crow lifted off and flew toward the edge of the In-Between. As soon as it passed the far side of the oaks, it vanished. Not even a fall of feathers marked its presence. It might never have been here at all. I could've been talking to nothing. Hallucinating.

"You saw the crow?" I asked.

"Here and then gone."

My voice shook. "We've got to get under cover."

Simone spun on her heel to take in the opposite side of the road. I followed her gaze.

A row of squat, windowless, red brick buildings lined the concrete. Their corrugated tin roofs didn't sit right, as if a construction crane or a movie monster had picked them up to look underneath and set them back down willy-nilly. The buildings stretched as far as I could see to our left. To the right, there were maybe five before the road dead-ended, one last building marking that spot. None of the buildings looked occupied, but looks almost always deceived. And if they were like the other buildings in the In-Between, some of them would be ordinary structures, solid and set on the inside. We'd walk in and what we saw was what we'd get. Some of them would be portals that led to other places in the In-Between. We'd step inside and find ourselves transported to another part of this world, with no way to know whether we'd land someplace safe or be dropped into danger.

No one came to the In-Between unless they had no other choice.

Simone's voice was bleak. "Which one?"

I reached for my fae instinct. It sputtered and then went out, like a cigarette cherry ground under a boot heel. "Can't tell."

"No more magic?"

I shook my head. "All out of gas."

She swallowed hard. "We're going to have to count on logic, then, and hope it works in our favor. Not the one at the end. Too obvious if someone comes looking for us."

"The crow said this place isn't safe."

"Nowhere is."

She started toward the second from the end, limping even though her legs ought to be fine. I gave her my good arm to lean on. She took it without argument.

Our shoes whispered on the concrete, shadows stumbling ahead of us. Even our breathing sounded unnaturally loud to me. Could Famine—or anyone else hunting us—hear all that racket? Could she smell us over and above the sulfur in the air? The days'-old dirt and the blood and the exhaustion?

Simone and I were sitting ducks.

I picked up the pace, half-dragging Simone until we reached the building she'd chosen. The door was made from unpainted pine, swollen and stubborn. It took some elbow grease before it opened on squealing hinges. Moonlight flooded the entry, lighting a path across the smooth, empty concrete floor.

It wasn't big on the inside, maybe as big as an apartment living room. A mound of packing blankets littered the far corner. A red metal mechanic's cabinet leaned against the wall. A long, flat stone with two inches' worth of candle wax sat in the center of the space like a forlorn altar.

No enemies hiding behind any of it. Not even a ghost.

"It's good," I said.

Simone shoved the door closed behind us. It had a deadbolt, and she used it, enfolding us in darkness. A moment and a rustling sound later, I heard a soft click. A wan halo lit her chin and the point of her nose. It took me a second to realize she was holding a flashlight.

"Batteries are dying. It loses a little something." She motioned with the head of the flashlight toward my pack, positioning the fading light so I could see inside to find a tin of matches.

I used them to light the two longest candle wicks. They sparked immediately, flames stretching tall, blue and smoky. Their light wavered and then steadied. In the candlelight, I could see how pale Simone had become, how her legs shook as she tried to remain upright, how her knees buckled as she backed up toward the closest wall. She slid down to sit, exhausted.

I yanked one of the moving blankets from the top of the stack, but she waved it away. I set it beside her for when she might want it.

"What's on the floor?" she asked.

White smears. Not tracked-in dirt, but chalk. Lines and symbols that had been carefully drawn, then destroyed. I didn't recognize the pattern exactly, but I could read the intent.

"A protection spell. At least, it used to be." It was elaborate, and it was a fae working, not a human one. "It's not a threat."

"But there was one," she said. "Or whoever made it in the first place wouldn't have."

The wheels in my mind turned. I tried to connect to the land and to magic again, reaching down and opening my heart. I found only the barest flickering spark of fae power, not enough to open another door between realms or even to defend against the attack I expected to come any minute. Maybe it was enough to help me see the threads of the protection spell on the floor.

The dusty chalk lines glowed ever so slightly, enough to make out the shape of a five-pointed star set inside a circle. A pentacle, a magical symbol representing the five elements of life—earth, air, fire, water, and spirit. Enclosed by a circle, the star became a form of protection. The lines of the star were whole and complete, but the surrounding circle was not. A section of it had been erased.

I searched the floor for chalk, upending the pile of blankets and the altar stone, busting through corner cobwebs. No joy.

I knelt beside the erased portion of the circle, dragging my fingertips over the chalk. Could the old chalk be brushed and stretched to complete the circle? My stomach sank. There was nothing left on the surface of the floor. The chalk had somehow been made a part of the concrete.

We didn't have chalk in our packs. We'd arrived in Faery with no supplies, so we'd scavenged what we could and traded for other essential items—water canteens, a flint, a decent knife. No reason to have spent valuable resources trading for something as useless as chalk.

*Think.*

What could I use to complete the line? What power could reactivate the spell when I had none to spend?

I stared at the pentacle. Earth. Air. Fire. Water. Spirit. The elements of life that made up all things.

What did we have in our bags? What did we have on our persons?

Fire and steel. Flesh and blood.

Simone's voice held an edge of panic. "Kevin, where are you?"

I glanced at her. She looked right at me, but her eyes were unfocused. She couldn't see me.

A fist of fear squeezed my heart. "Right here."

Her voice was soft and small, her eyes heavy-lidded. "I'm scared."

I'd never heard her sound like that before. "I'll make it all right. Promise."

It was a lie, but it seemed to calm her, thank God for small favors. She was getting worse, and she needed healing I didn't know how to give. I could look for help or supplies nearby, but I couldn't bring her with me if she couldn't walk or run. I couldn't leave her without protection.

I fished in my pack for the knife, closing my hand around its cool silver hilt. Once I had it in hand, I whistled, both hoping and fearing that the sound would be heard outside our four walls. I took a deep breath, praying for an answer, half-expecting Famine to break down the door. Instead, I heard only the rise of frog song outside. Bright silvered moonlight spilled through the seams of the building. The wind gusted. Wings caught on the breeze.

A black bundle of feathers burst through the far wall as if were made of nothing at all, pinpoints of light shining from its wings. It flew straight for me like a missile, not slowing, not stopping.

It was the same crow who'd warned me about Famine. It had been a friend—or acted like one. The hell was it doing? I threw up an arm to protect my face. The crow flapped its wings once.

My arm was high. It aimed lower.

It speared through my chest as it'd cut through the wall—as if there were no boundaries to my body. One second it was outside of me, the next inside.

I felt it move within me, clawing at muscle and bone and skin like an alien invader. It's wings seemed to fill my shoulders and arms, its head at my throat, its heart lined up with mine. My heartbeat became a low hum, the space in between each thump growing longer. I gasped for air, drawing it deep into my lungs, suddenly unable to exhale.

The silver knife tumbled from my hand, but didn't fall. It hovered in the air, the blade reflecting the candles' glow like a star in the dark. I tried to look at her, but my head refused to turn. I couldn't move a muscle. I couldn't even blink.

In the midst of all this stillness, my thoughts raced, trying to fill in the blanks, to find an explanation for what had just happened. For what was still happening.

A familiar voice rumbled inside my chest, rattling in my throat. It belonged to the crow, and it echoed in my mind. Two words.

*You called.*

I'd whistled, yes, intending to ask it for help. To plead with it to travel to the human realm and pass on a message to the one person who might be able to get us out of this mess.

I called up an image of him in my mind's eye. Bald head, pale skin, gray eyes that had seen millennia, black leather trench coat. The human form of the serpent from the Garden of Eden, Malek.

*I've sent for him,* the crow said.

How? The bird was inside me.

The picture of Malek's face in my mind washed away like a sand-castle struck by an incoming wave, only to be replaced by a different image: The single crow as part of a larger whole.

It had its own consciousness, free will, and magic, but it was also connected to the consciousness of all other crows. The crow within me had sent a message to another of its kind to travel to the human world and fetch Malek.

I was grateful, but felt no relief. There was a bird inside me, and I didn't understand how it had gotten there or why. I couldn't move or breathe. I couldn't protect Simone or myself. I was fucking helpless.

*It's worse than that,* the crow said. *You're fading.*

Fading? I felt fine. Simone was the one in trouble. It was just my magic that had taken a nosedive. I was fae and immortal and—

It hit me like a punch to the gut. I was fae. The fae were made of magic. If the spark of my magic had gone out, then the rest of me wouldn't be far behind. I would die, and there would be no one to take care of Simone.

*I can't let her die.*

*I did not come to help you with that.*

*Then why the fuck are you here?*

*To save you.*

That stopped me cold. I didn't need saving. I needed to save Simone.

*Stop fighting me.*

What else was I supposed to do when a magical bird invaded my body? *Get out of me.*

*If I leave, you die now. If I stay, I help you hold on.*

Stark words I didn't want to believe. But, because I was fae, I knew the crow told the truth. It lent me its magic, keeping me alive. Maybe it could make itself useful in other ways.

*Help me get the protections back up.*

I felt the wheels of its mind turn. I heard every thought. The crow hadn't stopped time. It had pulled me out of the flow altogether. Meaning that the world moved on without me. The crow held me in stasis, keeping me safe, but whatever was wrong with Simone continued to harm her.

The crow had done what it could, the only thing it could. Its mission was to ensure that I survived. Without me, there would be no one to help Faery.

Simone and I had come here to save the realm. I still wanted to do that even if I didn't have any idea how. But if I had to choose between Faery and Simone, I'd choose Simone.

*Help me heal her.*

*My magic heals, but not in the way you think of healing. I transport souls from one realm to the next.*

The crow was right. That didn't sound like healing at all. But even if it couldn't fix her, it could back me up.

*What you plan is unwise,* it said.

I didn't care what it thought or said. It wouldn't change my mind.

*Help me, or I won't help you.*

It heard me, loud and clear.

The spinning blade fell in slow motion, end over end, the tip hovering above the floor for an eternal moment before it struck with a ring of metal on concrete. The thump of my heartbeat sped up, pushing blood through my veins until the sound of it roared in my ears. I blew out a long breath, sucking in the next as my legs gave out and I dropped to my knees. I reached for the knife, fingers closing around the hilt.

Whatever magic I had left lived in my veins. The crow could boost its power.

I sliced the blade across my palm. Liquid light flowed from the wound, dripping onto the floor, filling the break in the chalk circle. With the circle whole again, I expected a flash of light or a peel of thunder, or even to feel something click into place, announcing that the protections were working. Instead, the smallest spark ignited in the back of my mind.

A hush descended inside the cabin that reminded me of the space between the night and the dawn, when the world felt balanced and still and perfect. Then, like the first of the sun's rays painting the horizon, light spread along the length of the circle, flowing into the five points of the star, rolling along the chalk lines until every inch of the pentacle glowed.

In the center of the star, the floor shimmered. One second, it was concrete. The next, the solid gray stone opened like an eye, awake and watchful.

I blew out a shaky breath and forced myself to stand, looking for any hole in the defenses, finding none. That didn't mean there weren't any, only that the circle was as strong as I could make it right now. It would keep out most anyone with ill intent who tried to enter the building.

I stumbled as much as walked toward Simone, scooping her up. She hung limp in my arms, a sheen of sweat on her forehead, her eyes heavy-lidded and unfocused. She was barely conscious, where only a few minutes ago she'd been able to talk.

The speed of whatever had made her this way terrified me. I moved as fast as I could, as carefully as I could, laying her down inside the circle without smudging a single line or edge. Retreating from the circle, panic swarmed inside me like angry bees. I slammed a lid on the rising emotion before it swept out of control, funneling wave after wave of it into a prayer.

Stealth. Silence. Nothing to see here. Nothing to feel.

I whispered the words over and over again in my mind, then murmured them aloud. The circle, and Simone within it, wavered in my sight.

Stealth. Silence. Nothing to see here. Nothing to feel.

The circle faded from the outside in, vanishing, taking Simone with it. I prayed until I couldn't see a single trace of either, until the space where they'd been moments before was just that—space.

They were still there, the circle and Simone, camouflaged and as safe as I could make them.

Help was on the way, provided that the crows got the message to Malek, that he was free to travel to the In-Between, that he could find us here—a lot of ifs. I was afraid to leave Simone, but I had to find a way to slow down what was happening to her. I had to stop it.

I started for the front door, but the crow inside me hesitated. Famine or anyone else after us would expect me to leave through the door.

Spinning on my heel, I walked toward the back wall, gaze skimming over corrugated metal, not understanding what I was supposed to do. Images flashed in my mind. The metal dissolving as if it weren't there. The sulfurous dark outside.

The crow had flown through the wall to reach me. Its magic allowed it to travel between worlds. To transport the souls of the dead from one realm to the next. It knew how to do what I did not.

I took a deep breath and stepped forward, counting the strides to the wall. One. Two. Three.

On the fourth, the wall swallowed me whole. For a heartbeat, I tasted iron and copper, felt the airless cold press against my skin, before it spat me out into the night.

# CHAPTER 3

THE ALLEY BEHIND the building was dark and empty. Gravel crunched under my sneakers as I shifted my weight from one foot to the other. Sulfur swirled on the wind, its stench coating everything with a hellish film and invading my lungs. Listening hard for the sigh of breath or the small sound or the errant thought that might betray a spy or another assassin, I heard nothing at all.

I was alone—except for the crow inside.

It shivered as the night air brushed my skin, whispering a word in my mind.

*Fly.*

If I did that, there would be no way to hide from prying eyes. Famine or her agents would only have to glance up to know exactly where I was—and they weren't the only dangers in the In-Between.

But the crow flew through the In-Between all the time. Unlike me, it didn't have to avoid walls and boundaries. It crossed them at will. And the crow was within me, lending me its magic.

I unfurled my wings and took off at a jog, leaping to catch the air, riding a low current. Instinct and logic demanded that I stay below the rooflines, where the space was tightest, where the tips of my wings passed within inches of walls. Flying such a fine line felt claustrophobic, like a fist squeezing my heart and lungs.

*Turn,* the crow said, its body tilting inside mine to guide me.

I banked right, eyes widening as a sped toward a metal wall. I squeezed them tight at the moment of impact—as the wall dissolved around me, revealing an interior that looked exactly the same as the one I'd just left, down to the stack of blankets and the mechanic's chest, but without the chalk on the floor. A thick hardback book sat in the center of the floor, gold embossing on the spine glowing in invitation. As I looked at the book and my gaze focused on the surrounding floor, I made out a network of barely visible lines like a spider's web. A trap, ready to be sprung.

That was all I had time to glean before I flew through the far wall, into the night, and through the next wall.

The new building held the same blankets and chest, but in this one an enormous dog lay in the center of the space, so big it might not be a dog at all but a wolf, white with brown eyes. It looked up at me and barked once, softly. Then, as quickly as I'd entered, I found myself outside again.

The in-and-out, the quickness of it, the strange, creepy vibe of the place was bewildering and disorienting. I squeezed my eyes shut again, this time to drive out that feeling, to concentrate on what I needed.

Medical supplies. Healing magic.

I calibrated my senses, calling up the memory of hospital smells, of what it meant to be a healthy human, all systems functioning optimally.

*Turn,* the crow said again.

I banked left and burst through the next wall and—into a black hole. It stole the air from my lungs and the spit from my mouth. It pressed against my skin like a thousand-pound weight, until I felt flattened and stretched and steamrolled.

Then the weight lifted as suddenly as it had come, and I crashed face-first into a hardwood floor. My nose slammed into the boards hard enough to make me see stars, but not hard enough to break it, thank God. My eyes watered, tears streaming into sawdust. When I sucked in a breath, I tasted oak and pine and sadness.

I swiped the back of my hand across my face. It came away bloody and dotted with snot. A knock incited me to push up on my knees, adrenaline through the roof. It came again, easy to recognize as a drilling woodpecker, working on a tree outside.

What kind of woodpeckers drilled trees at night?

That was the just the thing—it wasn't night anymore, not in the one-room wood cabin where I knelt. Morning sun streamed through the single window, so bright it made my eyes stream even more.

Morning? How could hours have passed in a single moment?

I couldn't have been gone that long. Simone's illness had sent her spiraling down fast. Hours lost meant she'd have gotten that much worse. She didn't have that far to fall.

I scrambled to my feet, the sunlight piercing my skin like knives, sucking air, coughing at the sulfur taste on the back of my tongue. Remembering that nothing in the In-Between worked like it did in other realms. The In-Between was a fever dream.

Maybe hours had gone by. Maybe it'd been only minutes. I had no way to know. I could only search for the supplies we needed and get back as quickly as I could.

I looked around, catching the faint shimmer of a degraded protective shield that clung to the log walls. A line of half-burned seven-day jar candles sat atop an inverted blue milk crate in the far corner beside two rolled sleeping bags, a piece of folded white parchment peeking out from underneath the dark green fabric. A six-inch layer of dust covered it all.

Someone had been staying here, but they hadn't been back in a while. The walls echoed with barely perceptible sounds. I heard them like murmurs in the corners of my mind, and they tasted like the ghosts of memories.

I shook my head to clear it. I didn't have time to linger, listening to someone else's psychic leavings. But a tingle started at the base of my spine, rising to the nape of my neck, catching in my throat. It wanted me to listen, to brush away the cobwebs, to pick apart the bits and pieces of sound and memory.

One step toward the door and the tingle became a lightning strike that rooted me to the spot. I could push it away. Ignore it. Get the hell out of here and get to Simone.

If I didn't listen and missed something crucial, what then? What if I made things worse? What if I turned my back on the information that would help me keep Simone alive?

I forced myself to be still, to take a deep breath and push it down through the soles of my feet and the floor, into the ground of the In-Between. I took another breath and pushed it through the crown of my head and the roof, up to the sky. I grounded and connected myself to the In-Between, right here and now. A third breath opened the space behind my heart. Whatever this place wanted so badly to share with me, I'd hear the intention and feeling behind it.

I let the murmurs inside, allowing them to grow louder and louder, until they became a kaleidoscope of sound and vibrant color. A face became clear in my mind's eye—ghostly pale, bright blue eyes, a silver ring through an arched silver brow, spiky silver hair. A girl. She was fae, and there was something very wrong with her.

Something vital was missing, something I couldn't put my finger on. I breathed deeper and let myself sink in to the image of her face and the bright sound and color of her thoughts. A name rose like a bubble floating to the surface of still water. Silver. Her name was Silver.

She was confused—that much was easy to tell. She felt like a brand new, just out of the box being, as if she'd just woken up to her life. Her memories went back only a couple of weeks, although she knew she'd lived much, much longer. She recalled nothing about her life—not her childhood, not her parents, not her friends, not even what she'd loved or feared or hated or hoped for. Her only friend in the world had told her she was royalty. A literal Faery princess.

Here in the In-Between, she hid from her people. Her father, the Faery King, had ordered her killed on sight.

The King was a douchebag, so in a way him putting out a hit on his own kid didn't surprise me. But I also knew he'd had another daughter who died at the hands of humans, and how much pain and grief he still felt about that.

He had obligations and rules to follow because of his station. It wasn't just a job; it was what he was. You couldn't be the king, much less the king of a magical world, without those things. For the first time, I wondered whether he paid too high a price.

Silver had tried to save the realm from the same sickness Simone and I had come here to fight, and, like us, she'd screwed it all up. She'd given up her memory to fix her mistake. Her people didn't know and the King and Queen didn't care. They were sick, and Silver would save them. If they couldn't be saved, she'd overthrow them.

Jesus.

The last thought echo tasted of the ubiquitous sulfur, but also of sunshine and pine and the fire between the worlds—she'd left the In-Between. Had she made it to Faery? Had she managed to cure her parents or had she gotten herself killed?

It was a piece of the puzzle as to why Simone and I hadn't been able to find a way to the King and Queen. I had no idea what that had to do with helping Simone, or why I'd needed to stick around to hear it all.

I refocused, taking a closer look at the candles—nothing there except wax and glass—and unrolled the sleeping bags, hoping to find something useful stored in them. The first disappointed, but I hit a jackpot with the second. A couple of protein bars from the human world, past their sell-by date. An unopened bottle of ginger beer. And a stoppered vial of something green with the thick consistency of gel —a fae elixir handy for cuts and scrapes. I could work with the elixir. It might not fix what ailed Simone, but it might buy us more time. I tucked it into my pocket.

I unfolded the parchment last, blinking at the charcoal sketches I found inside. Two faces. I recognized both.

My friend, Stacy, from the mass of curls on her head to the almond shape of her eyes, the wry crook of her mouth, and the ring in her nose. She was a powerful witch who favored colorful sweaters and broomstick skirts with funky tights, and she had a penchant for boiling things down to brass tacks that I appreciated and missed.

Malek, whose gray eyes held the memories of millennia. His mouth was harsh, with no trace of a grin or smile lines. In the drawing, he wore a black watch cap on his bald head, and a black duster. He should be on his way to the In-Between by now, bringing his don't-fuck-with-me seriousness and power into the mix.

From the corner of my eye, I caught a sharp movement near the window. But when I looked at it head-on, I saw nothing there.

The crow spoke up. *Not nothing.*

Whatever it was, it wasn't inside the cabin, not with the remains of the protective barrier still intact. I'd seen something reach in magically, checking the defenses.

*Let's fly,* I said.

*No.*

No explanation, just the single word backed by welling dread. I hadn't felt that from the crow before—not from any of its fellow corvids, either. These birds could fly through walls and time and worlds. What did they have to fear?

I could only think of one thing. A Horseman of the Apocalypse.

If Famine was outside the cabin, then we were fucked. I couldn't fight someone that powerful, even with my magic at full capacity. The crow had a better shot than I did at getting us out of here.

*The path is closed.*

There was no way out. No way back to Simone.

Famine wanted me. The crow had said so. If she wanted to break into the cabin, she could probably wiggle her nose or flick a finger and destroy what remained of the protections, not to mention shatter the cabin into a stack of splinters. No use hiding inside or trying to hold out.

If we couldn't run, fight, or hide, that left only one option.

I headed for the door again, no lightning to stop me this time. I turned the knob and pulled, expecting to see the sunlight and pines from Silver's thoughts, along with a giant black-robed skeleton sparking with power.

Hinges creaked. A shadow blocked the sun. I stood face-to-face with empty, evergreen-scented air. Then, I glanced down.

A little girl stood at the threshold. She looked about ten. A dark blue dress with red polka dots hung to her skinned knees, red tights and dark blue Mary Janes rounding out her wardrobe. She'd pulled her blond hair into pigtails tight enough to make my head hurt, green eyes shrewd behind her the tortoiseshell frames of her glasses.

I opened my mouth to say something friendly, like *hi* or *who are you?*, but my jaw snapped shut before I could utter a sound. Every hair on my body stood at attention, every inch of my skin crawling with revulsion. Over a little girl. A child.

She smiled, her teeth too big for her mouth.

A memory appeared in my mind as if I had summoned it: my mother's face. No, more than that. My mother, whole and alive the way she'd been years ago on a day I still saw sometimes in my dreams.

Mom had her brown hair cut in something she called a shag, and I thought it looked messy, but also good. Summer had streaked it with gold, like the flecks in her brown eyes. She smiled at me, her cheeks flushed from too much sun because she'd forgotten her hat and we'd been to the beach down at Galveston all day. She smelled of sun lotion and salt and a tinge of August sweat, and she wore a purple tank top with an unbuttoned, untucked long-sleeved denim shirt over the top because her sunburn gave her a chill in the air-conditioned house. She'd rolled down the hems of her faded, cut-off denim shorts for maximum warmth, but kicked off her flip-flops as I watched. They landed on the linoleum in the kitchen with a shower of sand.

Oranges that smelled like summer lined the sill of the window that looked out on the backyard, where the branches of the oak tree waved in the wind and a squirrel raced along the top of the wooden fence behind it. Newspaper covered the big, oval kitchen table whose chrome pedestal had been so scratched by dog claws that no one could see their reflection in it anymore. We'd lost our yellow Lab, Abby, two months, one week, and three days ago. She'd been fourteen and had cancer. My heart still hurt. I pushed the thought of her away.

Mom peeled the plastic off a pound of ground beef and dumped it in the hot cast-iron skillet on the stove. The meat sizzled. The rooster clock over the stove ticked off another minute. The air conditioning clicked on.

Mom's voice sounded like the crashing of waves. "You worry too much, Kevin," she said. "You keep working like you do, you're gonna get that academic scholarship and I'm gonna be so proud of you."

I'd always wanted one. I'd always wanted to go away to school. I didn't fit in anywhere and she knew it. She wanted me to go.

It was only later, after she died in the accident, after Dad went down the beer-soaked rabbit hole, that it became an obsession bordering on whatever was worse than obsession. Then I had to get out or die trying. But with Mom? It was different. It was the way it was supposed to be.

"Put some water up, will you?" she asked. "The noodles always take longer to cook. And take a jar of sauce out of the pantry? The one with the peppers."

"Diavolo," I said. "The Devil makes the best shit."

She rolled her eyes at my language, but she didn't give me any crap about it.

I grabbed the big aluminum stockpot from the cabinet by one handle and flipped it into the sink. I turned on the faucet and watched the water fill the pot and couldn't help the swelling in my chest because she'd said she'd be proud of me.

She only used that word when she meant it, which made for few and far between times. That made me hungry to hear it. If only I could, one more time. If only I could see my mother's face somewhere besides my memory.

If I could make this memory real.

I'd slipped into memory without even realizing—not something I did. Not on my own, at least. Someone had sent me into a visceral experience of my past, of a moment I wished I could get back.

I could get it back, after a fashion. I understood that I could choose to stay in the memory. Time would stop. The kitchen would always smell like the beginnings of spaghetti and my mom would always have sunburned cheeks and sand between her toes and she'd never leave. I'd never have to grieve again.

I watched my mom pull a wooden spoon out of the big drawer by the dishwasher and stir the meat in the skillet. She could always be this way.

The prospect of that, that it was even possible, felt like the electricity hovering and humming in the air before a storm, when the air is so charged you're sure it will catch fire. I felt that in every single molecule in my body. I'd never wanted anything so badly in my whole life. I'd never felt so hungry for anything.

If the little girl could give that to me, what price wouldn't I pay?

I wouldn't be the only one to pay it. Simone needed me.

At the thought, the whole of my mother—her sun-kissed hair and her smile and her gold-flecked eyes—started to fragment in front of me like glass broken into cutting shards. I could no more stop it than I could stop time.

I could never go back. My mother was dead, killed by a drunk driver late one night. The police had come. I'd never forget the sound of that knock on the door, or waking up groggy and pissed off about it, or feeling my legs give way and the harsh thud that shivered through my bones as I hit the floor, or the expression on my father's face and the hot, fat tears that'd run down his cheeks. I'd never seen him cry before, not ever.

Nothing had ever been the same, and it never would be.

I blinked, and the world seemed to right itself, the reality of the In-Between, rotten egg stench stinging my eyes. The girl in the doorway seemed to take up more space than she should, and her eyes had darkened from green to black.

She wasn't human. She wasn't fae. Not a demon or an angel, either.

"The hell are you?" I asked.

Rage erupted like a volcano behind her eyes. I tasted smoke and ash and fire and then she struck so fast, I never saw her hand move. But I felt the punch to my solar plexus hit me like a speeding truck, stealing my breath. The force of the blow knocked me off my feet, shoving me across the cabin. I landed in a tangled heap, skidding into the milk crate with a crash of glass as jar candles toppled like bowling pins.

My arms shook as I planted my palms on the floor and struggled to my feet, sucking air and raising my eyes to meet the gaze of the little girl who'd knocked me across the room. Pigtails, navy blue jumper, and Mary Janes. Awkward arms and legs too long for the rest of her body. The glint in her eyes was anything but childlike, though.

My vision blurred around the edges. Blinking didn't help. The girl seemed to move in slow motion, footfalls whispering on wood planks —then, as if someone had punched fast-forward, she closed the distance between us.

Her uppercut caught my chin with enough power to rocket me upward. I hit the ceiling hard, floating for a split-second before gravity grabbed hold. I braced for impact with the floor. It never came.

A Mary Jane barreled into my belly. I hit the wall. The boards cracked, opening wide like a hungry mouth that chewed me up and spit me out into sparse grass laced with pine needles. I rolled head over heels to a slow stop, a cloud of dust boiling into the air in my wake.

I tried to stand, but my legs refused to cooperate. I levered myself to my knees, then fell face first into the grass, heart racing. Any second now, the girl would strike again.

I couldn't take another punch or kick. And she'd been inside my head before that, invading and weaponizing my memories. She hadn't told me her name. She had demanded nothing.

I shouted at the crow. *Get me out here.*

The girl stalked through the shattered wall, her mouth a thin line stapled to her face. I read my death in her eyes.

Feathers fluttered in my chest, in my shoulders. The crow lifted me up, forcing my limbs to work. I staggered back, spinning precariously on my heel to walk and then run with a limp. Every breath seared my side. The crow spread my arms wide, unfurling my wings. It launched into the air, dragging my heavy legs. For a moment, I knew the drag was too great. That we'd fall like a stone.

Then my wings snapped, catching the wind. I didn't dare glance over my shoulder. I didn't matter whether she followed—only that we fled as fast as we could.

The crow flew us at breakneck speed through alleys, skirting corners of buildings and punching through walls. Anything to get away. Anything to throw off pursuit. The pulse of my own blood roared in my ears. My sense of direction failed completely. I had no idea which direction we flew or whether we doubled back as we shot from bright day to dusk to dark and back again. I didn't know how long we flew, only that we didn't slow until the malevolence at our back dissipated and finally disappeared altogether.

Did that mean the girl had given up? She'd done everything in her power to end me. She wouldn't stop until my heart did.

We flew low, skimming a gravel alley, shooting out into the night and bursting through a wall of sulfur and heat. Were we leaving or entering the In Between?

I glimpsed a familiar stand of oaks and the nothingness behind them. The boundary of the In Between near where I'd left Simone?

We banked, heading for asphalt-ribboned concrete, familiar metal huts rising from the earth on the left. I drew a shuddering breath as I counted the buildings and pinpointed the one with Simone inside. We banked again, heading straight for it. Then everything changed in the space of a heartbeat.

Our forward motion stopped on a dime, as if we'd flown into an invisible wall. We dropped fast and hard toward the concrete. I got my feet under me just in time to land in a squat, arms flailing for balance, the impact hammering my shins and my back.

*The hell?*

The crow didn't answer.

There was a hole where it'd been before. No more brush of feathers or flexion of muscle or murmur of its alien consciousness. I felt naked. Defenseless.

A few feet of road and walkway stretched between the door I wanted and where I crouched. My breath frosted the night air. A breeze rattled the bones of the oaks. Pressure built inside my chest and on my skin—nerves or danger? I heard no thoughts, but then I couldn't trust anything except the attempts on my life, on Simone's life. We were in deeper shit than I'd imagined, and I couldn't see a way out. If the homicidal girl found us right now—

Following that thought made me want to throw up. I shoved it away. I had to get to the door. To Simone. Without the crow, how would I get there? How would I make it past the magical shielding the crow and I had built?

Realization dawned slowly as if I were waking up from a deep slumber. I felt no magic within me at all. It wasn't just that the crow had abandoned me. Even the magical fae nature I'd gotten used to and depended on lately was just…gone.

I was human again.

A strange mixture of relief and terror bubbled in my gut. Relief, because I'd become me again. Even with the touch of magic that allowed me to hear thoughts in times of danger, I was a regular human with regular-sized emotions, like I'd been all my life until a couple of weeks ago. Terror, because I'd become powerless when Simone needed me most, with the deadly, murderous girl in the Mary Janes and assassins. With Simone sick. Dying.

My legs disobeyed every command I gave. If I wanted to move, I'd have to find another way. My legs wobbled and my arms shook violently, threatening to give out as I pulled and crawled one foot at a time toward the door. Gravel dug into my palms. With every breath, the pain in my side sharpened to a razor point. Bruised ribs? Broken? As hard as the girl had hit me, I could be bleeding internally.

With each passing minute, I expected to pass out. With every rivulet of sweat that soaked my skin and watered the earth, I expected the end to come. The whole world narrowed to the strip of ground in front of me, until suddenly there was no more ground, only the door.

I reached for metal. It was icy against my palm. The protections didn't attack me. I couldn't even feel them. Were they gone? Dismantled by the enemy? Had the girl or another assassin already broken in?

Adrenaline pushed through me, strong enough to help me reach halfway toward the knob. My fingers climbed the rest of the way, grasping the round shape of it. I held on with every last drop of will and turned.

A hush descended, sudden and so still I could no longer hear my own wheezing. Pressure built inside my head until I thought it would explode. My fingertips slipped through the knob, falling toward the face of the door and *through* the metal surface.

I stared, trying and failing to understand as my hand continued to slide through the door, disappearing to the wrist. I tried to pull it back, but the metal not only refused to let go, it yanked me forward, swallowing my arm to the elbow.

It was impossible to get my feet under me—impossible to get any traction at all with muscles that wouldn't obey my commands.

Another strong pull took my arm to the shoulder, shoving my face against the metal. It felt cold and dead. It had no mind of its own. It wasn't dragging me inside—someone or something else was. The girl?

My mind raced, sparking synapses trying to forge connections. No time to make a plan. No time to do anything except take a deep breath before the door swallowed the rest of me and spit me out.

# CHAPTER 4

I TUMBLED ONTO THE CONCRETE floor, rolling into the chalk circle, blurring sharp lines as I rolled to a stop, flat on my back beside flickering candles and their moat of melted wax. The ceiling spun sharp and wild, as if I'd downed my weight in alcohol. I squeezed my eyes shut and clutched at the floor, nails scraping the smooth surface with a zing that skittered along my spine.

Simone's whisper broke the spell. "Kev?"

I rolled in the direction of her voice, on the edge of throwing up. I swallowed hard, and both the urge to boot and the spinning faded. Once I could turn my head, I caught sight of her crouched with her back against the far wall, right where I had left her. Her eyes were glazed, no longer blue, but violet and glowing with fae power. She'd folded her gossamer wings behind her, their fine edges glittering in the candlelight.

"Sorry," she said. "I had to get you inside, but I couldn't make it to the door if I tried."

"Magic," I said.

"Magic."

I'd become human again, and she'd become fae.

"Rude must have shifted our world back to what it's supposed to be. Turned us back into what we were before."

That was the most logical explanation for what had happened, exactly what we'd hoped for. It just didn't matter right now.

I could no longer see the magical effects of the poison that worked inside her, but I read her body language just fine—the downturn of her lips, the trembling of her fingertips. Fine lines webbed at the corners of her eyes, pain writ on her skin. And I could hear her thoughts, molasses-slow.

"Did you get what you went out for?" she asked.

"Something for your wound. Yeah."

"Thank you."

She didn't look grateful. She looked afraid in a way I'd never seen before.

I pushed to my elbows and, with an act of supernatural will, slowly pushed upright. The muscles in my legs complained, but they functioned—easier with every step, as if they were remembering how to move. "You don't think it will work?"

She shook her head. "Not if the poison is what I think it is. It was meant for me, Kevin."

"But the assassin was after me."

"She wanted me out of the way."

With Simone dead, I'd be alone, grieving, vulnerable.

"How do you feel?" she asked.

"Like I've been hit by a truck."

"But not like you're poisoned."

The opposite, in fact. "I'm shaky, but getting better."

She met my gaze. "I'm not."

I closed the last of the distance, pulling the elixir from my pocket as I knelt in front of her. "You'll drink this anyway?"

She nodded.

I pulled the stopper and handed over the vial, watching her down it in one long swallow. The lines at the corners of her eyes began to ease.

"Knitting the wound?" I asked.

"Thank you," she said again, and this time she meant it.

I blew out a breath. "I hate to tell you that we've got more trouble."

A laugh escaped her lips. "Worse than dying?"

"A girl with more power than I've ever seen. She made me hallucinate, then tried to kill me."

Her brow furrowed. Questions bubbled in her mind, but she asked none of them. "Even with the wound healing, I can't run."

"Me neither." If we had a few more hours, I felt sure I'd be all right, but right now? Even so—even if I could—I wouldn't leave her.

She read that on my face, then twined her fingers with mine.

I squeezed her hand. "You said the blade was meant for you. What does that mean?"

"That whoever wants me dead went to a helluva lot of trouble. They had the blade blessed."

"Come again?"

"Blessed, Kevin."

"Like, by a priest?"

"No priest's blessing—or curse—could hurt me or any other fae being," she said. "Only a wish uttered from the lips of a loved one. It's a complicated spell."

"How complicated?"

"The right year, month, day, and time, all combined with the right phase of the moon and seven drops of blood from the heart of someone who loves you. Then they have to wish for you to be something so anathema to who and what you are that, if their wish came true, it will destroy you from the inside out."

"Jesus."

She looked up at the ceiling. "If it's not done exactly right, it's worthless."

"Why would somebody do all of that?"

"To make sure I die. To make sure it's painful. To make sure that no one can bring me back after."

Bring her back? "Resurrection? That's a thing?"

She nodded. "Also a complicated spell that very few people have the juice to pull off, or the willingness to pay the price."

I couldn't wrap my head around the possibility, much less how high the price would be. "We know someone who could do this?"

"Malek," she said.

"He's on the way."

"He won't get here fast enough."

"You don't know that, Simone."

She blinked back tears. "My murderer wouldn't have left that to chance."

I let go of her hand and cupped the nape of her neck. "You're not allowed to give up."

She searched my eyes. "How can you not?"

Because we'd saved my family and friends and the world together. Because she'd given up her human life to help me. I owed her a debt I could never repay. Because if we couldn't save Faery, we'd done it all for nothing.

I could've said any of those things. They were all true. But they weren't the whole truth.

What lay between us was simple, and as complex as the spell that threatened her life—beyond my having been with someone else when I'd met her, and that falling in love with Simone had meant hurting Amy. Simone was fae. I was human. She was as close to immortal as I could imagine, and my life was fragile and finite. My greatest fear was her normal, and mine, hers. How could we be together without causing each other more pain? But how could I walk away?

I could not. I would not.

"Because I can't imagine the world without you in it." I leaned in, touching my forehead to hers.

"Okay," she said.

I drew back to look at her, finding the barest hint of hope in her gaze. "Okay."

"What now?"

"Now we wait. Malek will be here." He'd be in time because he had to be.

She shivered as I moved to sit beside her, back to the cold wall. I wrapped an arm around her, sharing warmth.

We sat in silence for a moment before she spoke again. "It has to be my dad. The one who made the wish."

She had friends, but few people who understood her enough to love her more than they feared her. For that, she had me. And her father, the school counselor. Mr. Nance, no first name.

Salt-and-pepper hair, a fondness for pinstriped suits and ties, and tie-up dress shoes that always sported a mirror shine. Unlike some of the school administration, he actually seemed more interested in how the students were doing than in keeping them in line. He looked out for the ones in trouble, or those with "unusual circumstances," like me.

"You told him you were never coming back," I said.

"Clearly." She nestled her cheek against my neck. "He still didn't believe it was true."

"He didn't want to." Simone was his only child. He loved her, he'd lost her when the Faery King grabbed the reins of her destiny.

"I can never be who I was before—totally naïve about how the world works."

"Drinking too much, sleeping too little, spending your nights singing with your band in bars?"

"Human again."

I combed my fingers through her hair. "But you were."

"For a couple of weeks."

"You didn't want to talk about it—how it felt. Whether it was weird or brought up good memories or bad. You only wanted me to treat you liked nothing had changed."

"Nothing to say about a temporary, magic-induced condition."

"You had plenty to say about mine."

"Kevin, you knew nothing about being fae. You had to defend us, protect us. You needed a crash course in how to navigate Faery. We had to talk about that stuff."

I nodded. "Even so."

"I don't have the strength to move much, so I need you to look at me, Kev."

I angled my head to meet her gaze. The pain that rimmed her eyes was more than physical. "Did you wonder what would happen if Rude couldn't reverse the demon spell?"

"For about a minute."

"Every day?"

"Every hour."

I took in the enormity of that. The uncertainty. The intensity and the fear. "Did you hope?"

"I'd be lying if I said no."

She was fae again, so she couldn't lie even though she wanted to. I wanted to tell her I was sorry, that if I could give her back her humanity, I'd do it in a heartbeat. I said none of those things, because of how they would sound, like meaninglessness dressed up with pity.

"Your dad would never do anything to hurt you," I said.

"Desperation makes people do dumb things."

"Why would your father want you dead?"

She mulled the question. "I can't think of a single reason, no matter how angry he might be."

I didn't think Mr. Nance was angry. Mostly, he seemed sad. I didn't want to ask the question that bloomed in my mind, but I couldn't be the only one thinking it, because how did you get seven drops of blood from someone's heart?

I tried to make my voice gentle, so the words wouldn't hurt so badly. "Do you think they killed him? Would they need to?"

Her voice cracked. "I don't know."

"Do you have any tie to him—blood or heart—that would tell you?"

"I cut them, Kev."

Because holding on to them was too painful. I took a deep breath and blew it out slowly. "Who did this to you? Who sent the assassin? Who sent the homicidal girl?"

Simone mulled the question. "The girl—tell me about her."

"Maybe twelve. Big, black saucer eyes. Pigtails. Cartoon strong."

"You said she made you hallucinate?"

"About my mom. It was like being transported back in time, into a memory."

"A good one?"

My voice cracked. "The best."

"That's not a girl, Kev. That's a Famine."

She said the word as if it were a name and not a starvation event. "Who?"

"A Horseman of the Apocalypse."

"You're fucking kidding me."

"Sorry."

"The hell is she here for?"

"You, sounds like. The memory she dropped you into, it wasn't real."

"Then what was it?"

"Hell," she said. "Or one hell. There's a lot of them—places where souls can become trapped after the people they belonged to die, or where live people can get stuck going through the same pattern over and over again, trying to find or hold on to their hearts' desires."

"My mom isn't my heart's desire," I said.

"But you still miss her. You wish she were still alive. A lot of things would be different. Your dad wouldn't have started drinking or ended up in that mess with the Faery King. You'd never have met me."

I'd wished for most of that just like she'd wished she could remain human. Mom's death had been a source of grief and pain for so long. Of course I still missed her. Time had faded the feeling, turning it from too bright and too loud into something more like…watercolors.

"I'd still have met you," I said. "That was, like, fate."

She didn't disagree, but she didn't dwell on the subject, either. "Kevin, if Famine is here and she's after you…things are starting to make sense."

In what world? "Someone hired her the same way they hired the assassin? That same person tricked your dad into making a deadly wish?"

She shook her head, the movement so slight and delicate, it scared me. "No one hires a Horseman."

"She's in charge."

"Yeah."

"That's—" I bit my tongue. I didn't know any word that encompassed what I felt.

"Terrifying?"

"Close enough. How can we fight someone like her?"

Simone didn't answer. For a few minutes, I figured she was thinking, but then she went still and closed her eyes. I could barely feel her breath against my neck.

I shook her gently. She didn't respond.

"Simone?"

No reaction at all.

I moved as quickly as I could, pushing away from the wall, laying her down on the floor. I pressed a finger to the pulse point of her throat—what I felt was weak and thready. In the chill and silence and dead of night, with help on the way but no way to know when—it rolled over me in wave after crushing wave. I couldn't catch my breath. I couldn't think.

I had to do both. I had to do *something.*

I couldn't lean on my magic, but there was magic in Simone as long as I could keep her alive.

She'd tucked the blade that poisoned her inside her pack. I yanked the bag by a strap, unzipped it, and dumped the contents on the floor, sweeping away everything but the knife. The blade looked the same as when I'd had fae eyes—like plain silver, hardened and sharpened enough to use as a weapon. But Simone's father's wish lurked in its molecular structure, along with his heart's blood.

If the wish had to be made by someone who loved her, could be countered, or the spell slowed, by someone else who loved her?

My skin began to tingle and the waves of overwhelm fell into pools of energy beneath my feet. With every breath, every heartbeat, the energy rose through my body, from the soles of my feet through my legs, into my belly and chest, down through my arms to my fingertips, up through my throat and mouth, past my eyes and into my crown.

It knew something I didn't. A secret. A spell. It pulsed within me, demanding to manifest. I let instinct take over.

It was impossible to stab myself in the heart, or to draw seven drops of blood from it. But I could take blood from the skin over it. With the slightest pressure, the blade's razor edge cut and blood welled—plenty more than seven drops. Would that be enough?

I made six more cuts, each to the left of the one before. The number felt important. Essential.

Blood ran in rivulets down my chest and belly, soaking into the waist of my jeans. As quickly as it coated the blade, it soaked into the silver, as if the knife were made not only to kill, but to soak up the life force of whoever it struck.

The assassin had cut me with the blade. She'd cut my fae self. Which mean that the blade held my life force *and* the fae magic woven with it. I prayed I could contact it, that I could use it.

I focused my will on the ties of blood, the ties of the heart. I wished with my whole being—body and soul—to heal Simone. I pictured her in my mind's eye whole and strong and healthy. I gathered all of my heart into a single breath and blew it along the length of the blade, visualizing the silver absorbing the breath as it had the blood.

I made one slice over Simone's heart, hoping for the best outcome. Instinct moved my hand before reason could ask why—not one cut, but seven, a mirror image of my heart. She didn't wake or flinch or give any sign she felt the spell I sealed into her skin. I prayed to the God I'd been raised to believe in and any other gods willing to listen that this would buy her time. That it would buy her life.

The pulsing energy drained, flowing out on each exhale, until I bent to brace my hands against the floor, spent once more. It was all I could do to find my place against the wall again and pull Simone close, snug inside the V of my splayed legs. I lifted her inch by careful inch until her heart drew level with mine, humming softly.

No instinct rose within me, telling me to sing to her. I didn't need it to. Song was her first love. Her magic. If she somehow heard me— or her magic did—it might help her fight.

I watched over Simone, singing every song I knew, pouring every emotion I felt into every word, every melody.

Candlelight kept the shadows at bay as the night deepened. The concrete floor felt hard and cold, and the air chilled me to the bone even through the blanket. Seconds ticked by in time with my heartbeat and Simone's. I listened as hard as I could, picking out and identifying every single sound, no matter how small. If any thoughts that didn't belong to me entered my mind, I'd know. I'd be ready.

# CHAPTER 5

A BANG AND RATTLE at the door jarred me awake. Panic shot through me like a flaming arrow. I shifted my weight before I remembered fully where I was and why. Simone's warmth against my chest brought it all back.

Another bang and rattle and I understood that someone was outside, knocking like Famine had at the cabin. No way would she try that again. If she wanted in, she'd find a way without asking for permission to enter. That she hadn't done so already astonished me. Hard on the heels of that surprise, shame arrived in full force.

I'd fallen asleep while on watch.

Simone breathed more deeply, the rhythm steady and sure. She no longer looked so close to the edge. She was...sleeping. Sleeping hard, even with the noise.

I gave thanks to the whole world—to all the worlds. The relief felt so strong, it took my breath away.

With trembling arms, I moved her as carefully as I could, setting her down and tucking the blanket around her before I rose on stiff and screaming legs, my breath fogging the sulfur-soaked, icy air. Light streamed in through small cracks and holes in the walls I hadn't noticed last night. Dust motes as big as dandelion blooms floated in the air. And my head felt like a grape under the sole of a boot, stretched to the limit and about to explode.

I plucked the assassin's knife from the floor—better safe than sorry —and headed for the door, wincing at aching muscles. My sneakers squeaked on the concrete. The deadbolt felt like ice, and my fingers didn't want to work right for a second before I turned it. I opened the door to a gust of wind that smelled like bubble gum.

The girl in front of me blew an enormous bubble that popped like a gunshot. A dozen skinny brown braids floated around her head, hanging past her shoulder blades. Her steel-gray glasses sat halfway down her freckled nose. She wore an unzipped black hoodie over a black T-shirt with a great big Thor's hammer plastered across the front, skinny jeans, and black motorcycle boots so new they probably gave her blisters.

She carried a large purple messenger bag slung across her body with her name—BETH—embroidered on the flap, and a cardboard carry tray with three extra-large coffees in paper cups with plastic lids. They smelled like salvation.

"I sent for Malek," I said.

"Malek sent me." She balanced the cardboard tray and pushed her glasses into place with an index finger.

"You?"

"A lot's changed, Kevin. It's been a minute since you and the Singer left."

I squinted at her. "A minute?"

"Like, six months."

I gaped at her.

She curled her lip. "When was the last time you took a shower?"

"You're asking about hygiene?"

"You look like a horror movie reject. If I'd known there would be blood, I'd have brought you a care package with soap and deodorant and clean clothes and manners and aren't you gonna invite me in?"

I stepped aside to give her room to enter.

When I'd first met her, she'd been an overcurious, too-rich, too-bored girl at my school who fell in with Melody, the one who'd caused the demon apocalypse. Beth had helped summon the thing, for crying out loud, and the fae disease we were still dealing with. Malek had given her a choice: help us, or die. She'd chosen door number one, like anyone with a half a brain and a sense of self-preservation.

Six months ago. "How?"

"You know time moves differently here, right? Please tell me you know that."

"Yeah." I shut the door behind her. "I just didn't think—things are really messed up here. We've been hiding. And running."

"And almost dying?"

I nodded.

"I'm here because I'm apprenticed to Malek now."

"I didn't know he took apprentices."

"He doesn't. He just made an exception to save me from a terrible, no good, very bad death." She looked at Simone. "What happened to her?"

"An assassin with a blessed blade."

"Damn."

"You know what that is? A blessed blade?"

"Apprenticed," she said. "To a god."

"She's better than she was last night—or she seems to be. Can you tell when she'll wake?" Or *if* she'd wake. I held my breath.

Beth cocked her head. "There's still a hint of a shadow hanging around her, but it's dissipating. She should be dead, but she's going to be all right. Whatever you did—however you did it—you're a miracle."

I exhaled slowly. The air seemed to taste of hope instead of sulfur and coffee. "A miracle."

"Yeah. She should wake tonight, near as I can tell. The thing is, we have to move before then."

"Famine?"

She nodded. "I met her once before."

Spoken as if she'd run into a Horseman of the Apocalypse at the mall. "How'd that turn out for you?"

"Awesome."

"Really?"

She met my gaze with haunted eyes. "She tried to snare me in one of her hells. Spent a lot of time trying to figure me out, why I didn't smell one-hundred percent human anymore, where I fit into the big picture, blah blah. The big picture being the capital-A apocalypse, which is apparently going to happen sooner instead of later. Then, she tried to get to me by manipulating a couple of my ancestors into a hell so she could kill them there. You know, make it so I'd never be born." She held up the carry tray. "Latte?"

I shut the door and pried a cup from its holder. The coffee was hot enough that it burned the tip of my tongue. "You're still here. Clearly, Famine failed."

"Did I mention that she has hells?" Beth asked. "She only failed with my ancestors because Malek stopped her. It was close. He might not have come out on top. And considering who he is, that should tell you something."

Sure. That we were well and truly fucked.

"He said to tell you he'd be here as soon as he can," she said. "He has something he needs to take care of first."

"Tattoo appointment?"

"Child care."

"Come again?"

"My ancestor, the one he managed to get out of that hell dimension—she's kinda young. Like, ten. Also, she mostly speaks Polish."

I stared at her.

"Anyway, you don't call. You don't write. People worried you were, like, dead in a Faery ditch. I called your dad and told him you were among the living."

Thank God. "Did you tell anyone else?"

"Rude is also pissed, but he'll get over it faster than your father. He gets the stakes."

That made me feel marginally better. I needed to ask about my ex —I needed to know what had happened to her. I just didn't know how.

Amy didn't have magic when our city turned into a demonic wasteland. She wanted to help, so she went to Malek. I still wasn't clear on what passed between them, only that he gave her a tattoo that allowed her to breathe under water. She'd gone into the bayou for a crucial spell component that made it possible for us to defeat the demon, but she'd refused to come out of the water.

I couldn't shake the feeling that it was all my fault. She'd felt useless. I loved both her and Simone, and, without realizing it, I'd made my choice. Simone came first, and Amy knew it.

"Don't be an asshole," Beth said.

"Excuse me?"

"Okay, so you were an asshole before to Amy, but she makes her own choices, too. You couldn't be her boyfriend. Don't try to take away her agency, too."

No one had ever said something like that to me. "Where's that coming from?"

"The thoughts written all over your face." Beth set the coffee down on the floor and sat down cross-legged beside it, lifting the strap of her messenger bag over her head so she could set the thing down. "Amy is incommunicado with most of us. Rude and the rest of them checked up on her for a while, but she got tired of people always asking whether she's okay. Before you ask, no, she never asks about you."

I winced.

"Not sure what you expected, but you should let it go. If it helps, she still talks to Malek."

She'd talk to the serpent, but not to any of her friends? "How does that help?"

"She's a mermaid, Kevin. No one else understands her. At least Malek lets her be who she wants to be without trying to make her fit into a box."

I hadn't done that. Had I? "What did he charge her?"

"Nothing."

"He never charges nothing." The price was always too high.

"I would know, wouldn't I? End of discussion." She unzipped her bag.

The sugar and dough scent that wafted out nearly drove me to my knees. "Donuts?"

"A dozen glazed from Christie's."

The hole-in-the-wall down the street from Malek's, where they made the freshest-tasting everything. I sat beside Beth, feeling as if the world had turned upside down.

"What happened to the assassin who cut the Singer?"

"She's dead."

"Good."

No uncomfortable facial expressions. No questions about the circumstances that made killing necessary or fascination with the gory details. Not even an "I'm sorry." Just approval. I didn't know Beth well, but from what I did know of her, that kind of response was out of character.

Apprenticed to Malek? More believable by the minute.

I took a donut from the box, the glaze cracking under my fingers. I shoved the entire thing into my mouth, an icy layer of fear and loneliness and worry inside me melting as surely as the sugar and dough melted in my mouth.

She took the box from me, pulled out a sticky sheet of wax paper, and spit her gum into it. She crumpled the paper and shoved it in the pocket of her hoodie.

"The boss should be here inside half an hour. He gets here, we go."

"And if Famine or another assassin shows up before then?"

"I got you."

Beth versus a Horseman of the Apocalypse. She'd already fought Famine once and lived to tell. But I couldn't see it. I couldn't reconcile what I knew about her with the girl siting next to me.

"You have Malek's blood magic?"

"Yeah, but it's more than that. I'm developing my own spells. And I'm his representative. You know, like, an extension of him? He always knows where I am and how to find me. He hasn't tried it yet—that I know of—but he can act through me, too."

"You mean, like, take over?"

"In theory." She glanced at her hands, studying her nails.

"Where are we going when he gets here?"

"I'd say the shop, but I get the impression he has somewhere else in mind."

"He didn't tell you."

"Either he hasn't thought much about it yet or he doesn't want me to tell you something before he's ready for you to know it." She plucked a donut from the box and dug in, looking anywhere but at me.

"You can't keep your mouth shut."

"I acknowledge the problem. I'm working on the problem."

In that way, she was exactly the same girl I'd met during the demon-pocalypse. "We're going into Faery."

"How do you know that?"

"I don't," I said. "But that's what makes sense. Things are still messed up there. If we don't get them under control, all the other worlds are screwed."

"I don't know a lot about Faery. Not yet."

"Crash course."

"Like you," she said.

I nodded.

"I'm learning all kinds of stuff I never thought I would, like how to deal with living forever."

I met her gaze. This time, she didn't glance away.

Her tone was as light and dosed with sarcasm as always, but rough around the edges. "When Malek took me as an apprentice, he marked me with his blood. That means he always knows where I am because blood calls to blood. Also, that mark means that other gods will automatically know I'm claimed. And as a special bonus, that also means my regular life is over and I can forget about all the stuff I ever wanted to do or be, because now I only have one path: Malek's. Eternity has a special, horrible ring to it. Doesn't it?"

"You're alive, though. You said saved your life."

"It's why I don't complain more. So what's the deal with Famine and the realm of Faery? There's got to be a deal."

If Famine had sent the assassin and arranged for the blessed blade, and if she'd done all of that to get Simone out of the way and kill me—as much as I wanted to think it didn't make any sense, that I was nobody special and nothing at all in the grand scheme of things, I had to face the facts as I understood them.

I'd have been dead a while ago if the Faery King had been willing to kill me. I was a thorn in his side and pain in his ass, and he considered me an outright threat to him, personally. But he'd refused to take that one final, decisive action because I was important to the realm. Faery needed me.

I still had no idea what for or why. I'd been too busy learning what it meant to have magical power and fighting enemies to figure that out. Now, I felt sorry for having put that question on the back burner, because now it mattered.

"If Famine is after me, she's after the realm." As I spoke the words, the tumblers in my mind fell into place, unlocking a cascade of thoughts. "This is about fate."

"Going to need you to unpack that for me, Kevin."

"Fate. You know, destiny?"

"I think those are two different things. One of them you have no choice about, and the other is all about choices. If it's your fate, it's written ahead of time. If it's destiny, then you decide whether you're walking that road or whether you'd rather take a detour. Anyhow, I don't believe in either of them, but especially I don't believe in fate. Because, fuck that."

I sympathized, but we weren't talking about personal fate or personal destiny here. "Doesn't matter whether you believe in it. It believes in you. The fae influence everyone's fate—the fate of entire worlds. If someone were to slip in and muck around with that—I mean, it's already on its way to screwed up because of the disease—the consequences could be catastrophic."

She tossed the half-donut she held back into the box and wiped her hand on her jeans. "No place should have that much power."

"I didn't make the worlds." But she was right. I'd bet that if Simone were awake, she'd agree, too.

The fae had their own story about how the world was created, and it had nothing to do with seven days and an old white dude with a beard who uttered a word that brought the world into being.

The fae said that, at the beginning of all things, when the Earth was a super-heated rock cooling over millions of years, an angel fell in love with the planet and its potential. Because of that love, the angel fell into the center of the Earth, where he slept and dreamed all of life into being. His name when he lived among the stars had been Lucifer. After he fell, he became known as the Dreamer in the Land.

His dreams flowed out of his body on his breath, and his breath rose through all the layers of the Earth—all the realms of the Earth— including the realm of Faery, where those dreams were shaped before they flowed into the Human world. It was only in the Human world where those dreams took on form, where they became people and animals and plants and rocks and every other thing in creation.

That was the brass ring definition of fate if I'd ever heard one.

Famine had to be here for that reason, and that reason alone. No matter how "necessary" I might be—I drew the line well before adjectives like "special," because I was just a person like everyone else, no more and no less—in the end, this wasn't about me at all.

"Famine's a player in the Apocalypse, and she wants to get her hands on the strands of fate," I said.

Beth held my gaze, her face uncharacteristically solemn. "We can't let that happen."

Another knock on the door made my adrenaline spike again. Before I could stand, Beth rose and tugged on the knob. The door swung open, hinges protesting, and above Beth's snaking braids I glimpsed a pale, bald head, gleaming in the morning light.

Malek. I couldn't see the rest of him, but I felt the rage radiating from him as if he could go thermonuclear any minute. I pushed to my feet as Beth stepped out of his way.

He smelled musty, like ancient texts and engine oil and reptile scales heated under a noon sun. His motorcycle boots were scuffed as hell. The hems of his faded jeans were frayed, but his black leather duster didn't have a scratch or a tear. His black tank had small, white fingerprints on the front. It looked like—

"Is that milk?" I asked.

He looked down at the stain, then raised his hands to sign. *Be glad it's not blood.*

Because that would be so much more natural. "What, my blood?"

*You don't call. You don't write.*

"Beth told me already."

*You know you're in over your head.*

Truer words. "I've never not been in over my head."

*This is different.*

"It's always different."

*Not this time. We need to move.*

"Beth told me."

*Don't waste any more of my time, then. And don't waste your time. You don't have enough left.*

Comforting. "Is it safe to move the Singer?"

Beth cleared her throat. "Ask her."

I turned to look and caught sight of Simone pushing up on her elbows. I closed the distance between us, kneeling at her side.

"How am I still here?" she asked.

I opened my mouth to answer, but Beth spoke before I could.

"Your boyfriend is resourceful."

Simone met my gaze. "He's something else, all right. You look like crap, Kev."

"I've been told." And I didn't care. The only thing that mattered was that she was all right. "Can you sit?"

She seemed uncertain. "Help me?"

I pressed a hand to the middle of her back and gave her the other to hold on to. She gripped it extra tight.

Beth handed Simone her coffee. "Cold, but caffeinated."

"You're a goddess," Simone said.

Beth blushed. *"De nada."*

Simone took a long sip, giving herself a milk mustache in the bargain. As she wiped it away with the back of her hand, she gave the place the once-over, eyes narrowing. "Malek, are you seeing this?"

His gaze roamed over the remains of the chalk circle and the puddled wax of the candles. In response, he didn't sign to Simone. He signed to me.

*What did you do here?*

"A protection spell. I was fae at the time."

He shook his head. *Something's not right about it. Something's not you about it.*

"The crow," I said. "It flew into me."

Malek raised a brow.

I didn't understand the problem. "Without it, we wouldn't have stood a chance."

He studied me. The closer he looked, the more my skin itched. *That kind of thing doesn't just happen.*

I shrugged. "Weird things happen to me all the time."

*It doesn't happen to anyone.*

"What do you want me to say?"

Malek shook his head.

There was nothing I could say, or it didn't matter, or both. Whatever. "When are we leaving?"

*Now.*

I looked at Simone.

"I'll be fine," she said. "Just need to repack my bag."

Because the contents remained where I'd dumped them on the floor last night. "Sorry."

She glanced at Malek. "Can you two give us a minute?"

Beth rolled her eyes, then headed for the door. Malek followed her. I heard their footfalls, but didn't turn to watch. I kept my gaze on Simone's.

She waited until the door closed behind them. "What did you do, Kev?"

Not a question I'd expected. "Is this about the protection spell or the crow?"

"Saving my life."

"I wished you well."

"Using your blood."

I nodded.

"It shouldn't have worked."

"It was the only thing I could think of. I didn't have any other magic."

"That's not what I mean." She downed the last of her coffee, setting down the empty cup. "It shouldn't have worked because there's no way to break the spell of a blessed blade. Once it's cast, that's it."

I didn't believe in no-win scenarios, and I didn't believe in giving up. "There's always a way."

"There's not. Magic isn't getting everything you want—or saving everyone you want to. And if you do somehow make it work, the price can be too high. There's a reason I don't want to see my father, and it's not because it hurts him to see me so different from the human girl who was once his daughter, or because I miss being human so badly, the regret is like ashes in my mouth."

"But both things are true. You told me so."

She didn't deny it.

"You held something back."

She nodded. "Being in relationship, being connected to someone else—it has consequences. Magical consequences. The right person can use those connections to hurt you."

"Famine got to your father and used his connection with you to hurt you."

"No, damn it."

She wasn't worried about herself at all—or she was more worried about her father than anything else. "Famine used your connection with him to hurt him."

She blew out a breath, lifting strands of hair from her forehead. "Do you see where I'm going with this?"

"You're worried about me."

"And your dad and your friends. Kevin, this is bad. Things are changing. There's a Horseman of the Apocalypse now, and assassins, and things that should be magically impossible are happening. The solid ground underfoot is disappearing."

I laughed. I couldn't help it.

She glared at me. "What's funny?"

"It's not," I said. "It's just—what seemed like solid ground to you has always felt like quicksand to me. You can say it's because I didn't know any better, but I think I know enough. I think we never could take anything for granted."

"Then what have I been doing all this time?" she asked.

Pretending? Wishful thinking? No, it was more than that. "Reacting. The world throws shit at you, you dodge, you fight back. But that's all it's ever gonna be if we keep reacting."

She considered for a moment. "You want to go on the offensive."

"You okay with that?"

She nodded.

"You afraid?"

"Aren't you?"

"Terrified." Although nothing felt as scary as last night had. "I should help you get your pack back together, seeing as I was the one who dumped it out in the first place."

I crawled across the floor, gathering lip balm and hairpins, matches and protein bars into a pile. There was nothing in the mix except the mundane stuff that made life more comfortable. Except a small square of white cloth tied with thin, red thread. Something about it warned me away. I didn't want to touch it.

She plucked it from the floor.

"It's a spell?" I asked.

"More like a...memory."

"Wrapped in a spell."

She flashed a wry grin. "I wanted it just for me, protected from prying eyes, and from time."

Whatever memory it was, it was important. Too important to leave behind in Faery. "This is why you wanted to go back for your bag."

She twisted the thread around her index finger. "I've had it since I was a child."

"Okay," I said.

"That's all?"

"You want me to ask you what's in it?" I wanted to know badly, because knowing would tell me more about her—what she wanted most, what she wished for. "When or how or whether to tell me at all is your decision."

She tucked the packet into her pocket.

Disappointment weighed a little heavy in my heart, but I wasn't about to let her see it. I concentrated on pushing her stuff into a pile and helping her reload her pack, then slung it over my shoulder, along with my own.

"I can carry that," she said.

"You're still healing." I tipped my head toward the door. "Ladies first."

She shook her head. "Together."

I gave her my hand to hold. She twined her fingers with mine as we made our way outside. Her skin felt a little warmer than usual, but not hot enough to alarm. Her legs held steady, her steps close to her normal gait.

As we moved across the threshold, Beth stepped back inside. She looked small and feral all by herself in the big room. She glanced over her shoulder at her boss.

*No trace, Beth*, Malek signed.

Beth touched a mark on her right arm just above the elbow— a tattoo in the shape of a peacock feather—and closed her eyes. Two seconds later, a breeze whipped up inside the building, lifting the blanket back onto the stack where I'd taken it from, brushing away any evidence of our footprints. The carry tray and empty cups vanished as if they'd never been there. The flecked blood from Simone's hair and clothes, and my magic, gathered into a rusty ball and *poofed* out of sight as well. The burnt candles and melted wax faded away. The circle faded to a dull mark.

By the time Beth rejoined, you'd never have been able to tell we'd spent the night under that roof—not physically, anyway. And I'd bet a cool million not magically either.

"You're gonna have to tell me how you did that," I said.

She shook her head. "You don't want to know."

"Really do."

She looked at me. Something about her eyes bothered me. So serious.

*You can argue about it later,* Malek signed. *Grab hold of me and don't let go.*

We did what he asked. His arm felt like iron inside the leather sleeve of his coat.

The asphalt-veined concrete, the stink of sulfur, the cloudless sky, and the bright sun that lit the leaves of the oak seemed extra real—more solid underfoot, thick enough to choke a person, impossibly blue and blinding. I could make out the dull scratches on the individual bricks that made up the building we'd slept in. I could almost taste the look in Beth's eyes that made me wonder what the hell she'd done to erase our tracks, and what the hell had been done to her that she could do such a thing.

Malek's blood magic.

I linked my arm through Malek's. Simone threaded her arm through mine and drew me close. I imagined I could hear her heartbeat, and that it sounded weak. It had to be imagination, didn't it? I glanced at her.

She looked right back at me. "What?"

"I'm hearing things," I said.

"Thoughts?"

"No. Your heart."

Her gaze turned speculative. "That shouldn't happen. It shouldn't be possible."

"Why not?"

"You're human," she said.

If there was more to it, she didn't have a chance to tell me.

The In-Between disappeared with a pop as we stepped between worlds, into and through the fire.

# CHAPTER 6

THE FLAME SEARED away the sulfur stench and any thought I had except when I could take my next breath. I clenched my teeth as sparks from the flame singed the ends of my hair and the threads of my jacket, blasting my skin. Pressure built in my chest and head. My vision fuzzed gray.

I tightened my grip on Malek and pulled Simone closer. A heartbeat later, the portal spat us out.

I sucked in air that tasted of crushed grass and rising sap and life reaching up from the earth with so much strength and determination, tears pricked the corners of my eyes. In place of concrete, I caught my balance in dark, rich soil deep and soft enough for my sneakers to sink into. Twilight painted the sky. A chorus of insect and frog song told me that no strangers lurked in the shadows of the forest that surrounded us.

I let go of Malek's arm, but kept hold of Simone's. Her knees buckled, although they didn't give out. And she breathed too fast, her heart continuing to race.

Beth's grin lit her face. "No ambush. This bodes well, don't you think?"

Overhead, a cawing crow answered her question. Interested and marking our presence, but not coming any closer for the moment. And how the hell did I know that, exactly?

Beth laid a hand on my shoulder. "Eyes sharp, Kevin."

"There's no one else here."

"Maybe no assassins, but no one else? That's not really true."

No, it wasn't.

We'd landed in a different part of Faery than the Forest of Dreams where Simone and I had been last. There were plenty of hemlocks and Doug firs, but also oak and holly and birch and yew—and every kind of tree I'd ever heard of, along with some I didn't recognize at all. I'd never seen a forest in my world where they all grew in one place. I'd never known that to be the case anywhere.

Except there was one place even in Faery where that kind of thing could happen: the home of the King and Queen. The Faery Court. The woods here were called the First Forest. Legend had it that these woods were as old as time itself.

I'd been here once before, when I rescued my friends and my dad. Then, I'd arrived on a teleporting bus, and I hadn't known anything about Faery at all.

A breeze kicked up, rushing through leaves and needles, swaying branches and spiraling moss and twigs and chipped bark off the ground. The trees seemed to whisper to each other just before the forest blurred, then lines and boundaries reasserted themselves, but in different places than they'd been before.

"Did the trees just move?" Beth asked.

Simone answered. "Don't worry about it."

"You're kidding."

"I'm not. It's normal."

A path appeared in front of us, a ribbon of cleared earth winding through the trees and over a small hill. I couldn't see beyond the rise, but I knew that, on the other side, sure as I lived and breathed, there'd be a gate that led under the ground into the place the King and Queen —no, the new Queen, Silver—called home.

I cleared my throat. "Malek? How did you bring us here?"

He squeezed Beth's hand gently until she let go of him so that he could sign.

*Safest place in Faery.*

"How, not why. We haven't been able to come here ourselves."

*Silver's consolidating her rule. There are factions arrayed against her. It's chaos. She's careful about who has the keys to the kingdom.*

Things began to make sense. "You're on her invitation list, but the Singer and I aren't. We've never met, but it's not like we're unknown."

*Silver's memory is...*

"She traded it to save her people. I know."

*How do you know that?*

"She told me. Or the cabin where she stayed in the In-Between did. There was an echo there that I picked up on."

*She knew you before the trade.*

But not after. "She trusts you?"

*Ask her yourself.*

Malek started down the path. He stepped on twigs and small stones and the occasional fallen leaf, but he didn't make a sound. Beth scrambled after him, braids swinging. She made every noise her boss didn't.

Simone and I brought up the rear. Her legs were a little shaky at first, but steadied as we went, even as we climbed the small slope. And her breathing evened out, heart slowing to something that sounded more normal.

"I'm all right," she said. "So, stop looking at me like I'm going to shatter."

"There could be side effects from the blade that my spell didn't fix."

"Yeah, there are."

I looked at her. "But—"

"You were listening before when I told you that there were consequences for magic, that there are some spells that can't be undone, right?"

"Heard every word."

"Then believe you made a miracle happen, but that doesn't mean there won't be fallout. We're just not going to know what it is for a while until things settle out."

"I don't like it."

"Magic doesn't care, Kevin."

That was a slap in the face, and it stung. "Harsh."

"But true. It's not just that I need you to understand. You need to really get it, Kev."

Because we were walking into the unknown, and the stakes felt higher every minute, and the decisions we made might have consequences we couldn't predict.

The trees crowded closer to the trail as it wound uphill, painting the ground with dappled shade. I breathed a little deeper, a little easier, as if the forest wanted me to.

Simone leaned close. "It's better here."

"Because of the magic?" I asked.

She nodded. "The ground under my feet—this ground—it's feeding me now."

Thank God for that.

Silver might not remember us, but she'd been a friend. Maybe we'd find shelter here. Protection. Maybe a home base where we could work out what we needed to about who was hunting us and put a stop to it. Then we could work on healing the realm.

We reached the top of the rise. From here, it was easy to see the large, hollowed out cairn of stones down below and the short, silver gate that blocked its low front entrance. The stones had stood in the same place for so long, grass and moss should've grown on them, but they remained bare. Magic flowed off them in waves so strong, I felt them like real ocean waves. The unexpected power, enough to knock a guy off his feet. The tidal pull, the undertow.

There would be guards in the treetops. There always were. I glanced up, looking for them, but saw none—not that they made a habit of being conspicuous. They were there in case of trouble, and it was always better to get the jump on trouble. All four of us were known quantities. No need to check IDs at the gate or ask questions. No need to call down a greeting. But it bugged me all the same even with the perfectly logical reasons.

Malek led us down to the gate. The slope was steeper than it looked, making it harder to watch anything except where I placed my feet, or face tripping over tree roots that buckled up through the earth or stones that suddenly seemed to appear. Our footfalls kicked up puffs of dust—all except Malek's, anyway. The earth on either side of us rose gradually to knee-height, turning the path into a ditch. By the time we reached the gate, that ditch felt claustrophobic.

The gate itself, which had looked short from the angle at the top of the hill, revealed itself to be about seven feet tall up close. No ornament, just plain silver bars magicked together, except for the delicately wrought oak leaf at the center.

Malek studied it for a long moment.

"What?" I asked.

He turned his body so I could see his hands. *Nobody has opened this. Not in a while.*

Simone squeezed my arm, then let go. "Define 'a while.'"

*Months.*

"When did you last see Silver?" I asked.

*When I inked her. In April.*

Three to four months ago. What were the odds no one had entered or left the Court in that time? "What did you ink her with?"

*That's between her and me.*

Simone stepped in front of me. "We should get inside now. Malek, move."

He blinked at her command, but did what she'd asked.

I realized I hadn't seen her and Malek interact much with each other except during dire emergencies. As two magical beings living a couple of miles apart from each other, they had to have known each other before I arrived on the scene. Clearly, they didn't follow a god-versus-everyone-else hierarchy in their dealings.

Simone slipped past him and placed her palm on the oak leaf. She sang a phrase. It took me a second to recognize the language as Irish Gaelic.

*Oscail do shúile.*

A shock flew through me like a streak of lightning, sparking from the base of my spine and racing through the top of my skull. Judging from the way the others straightened up and the glances they gave each other, they felt it, too. The magic of Simone's voice, of what she was, wove with the power in her extraordinary voice.

Malek looked at her with outright envy. I caught the naked expression on his face for a split second before he shuttered it. When he was made at the beginning of time, he'd been able to do what Simone did with plain words rather than song—until he'd tempted one too many humans and the being more powerful than him cursed him, taking his ability to speak.

The gate unlocked with a click and swung in.

"What's that mean?" Beth asked Simone.

Simone glanced over her shoulder. "Open your eyes."

"Kind of weird, isn't it?"

"Not if you think about it," Simone said. "Follow me, and stay close."

I went in behind Simone, with Beth at my heels and Malek bringing up the rear. Passing through the gate was like walking into a dark house on a brilliant, sunny day—I couldn't see a damned thing. I could hear the tap my sneakers made as the ground we walked on shifted from earth to stone. I felt the hardness, and the seams between the shaved slabs of rock underfoot. The temperature dropped a good ten degrees. A spot between my shoulder blades chilled and set off a shiver. I took a deep breath of cool, damp air.

The pitch black all around started to separate into shapes and colors until I could grasp the outlines of burnt-out torches in their sconces set on either side of closed double doors, the faery version of a porch light. There should've been two guards here, but there was nobody at all.

In front of me, Simone froze.

I opened my mouth to whisper, then snapped it shut again when she reached a hand back and signaled silence. I tensed, waiting for someone or something to charge out of the corner shadows, but no one did.

Simone let go of the breath she'd been holding. "It's empty."

I spoke low. "The room?"

"The whole royal Court." She looked over her shoulder. The corners of her mouth turned down and her eyes were wide.

"We should check it out," I said. "Make sure, right?"

She swallowed. "Yeah. Make sure."

But there was as much hope in her voice as in mine: none.

If Silver and her Court weren't here, where were they? There was no such thing as a second house with these people. The whole realm was governed from this spot. Which meant that most likely there was no governing happening at all. What the hell was going on here?

"Silver wouldn't abandon her people," Beth said.

Simone nodded. "No. She wouldn't."

"Malek agrees."

"How can you tell?" I asked. It wasn't as if we could see his hands move well enough to read his signing.

"Remember that blood bond thing I mentioned before?"

That was just goddamn creepy.

Simone marched toward the double doors and pulled them open easily on their well-oiled hinges. The long corridor on the other side was dark and silent.

Our footfalls echoed as we made our way through the long hall. I could barely see Simone in front of me. The air was still, the sense of dampness more pronounced. If it got any more humid, water would condense on my skin. I stretched out my right hand, trailing my fingers along the wall, trying to feel when the corridor began to open out, the space expanding.

Simone stopped dead. I noticed in enough time to keep from running into her, but not to keep from tripping over my feet and flailing into the wall, knocking a torch from its sconce. It clattered to the floor while Simone turned and opened the first of the doors off the corridor. These rooms belonged to guards.

There were no lights in this room. No people, either, as far as I could tell. And so it was for all the rooms leading up to the end of the corridor. The echo of our steps seemed louder, as did the sound of our breathing. And Simone's heartbeat, which stuttered between beats. No heart should do that.

I sped up my pace until I came even with her, meaning to take her hand.

She grabbed for mine first and squeezed. "Kev. Look."

Straight ahead twenty feet, and impossible to miss—a long strip of flickering light filled the space underneath the doors to the great hall.

Simone and I walked shoulder to shoulder toward them, pushing them open together, squinting and blinking at the brightness. Torches burned in their wall sconces every few feet along the walls, casting the river-stone floor in ever-changing pools of light and shadow. The warmth of the fire washed over us, like coming home after a long time away, which was not a feeling I'd ever associated with this place.

Small, round tables flanked the sides of the football-field-sized room. They'd been draped in white tablecloths and decorated with low glass bowls filled with floating red and white roses. Red and white tapestries, also covered with what appeared to be live roses, hung from the walls. The perfume of the flowers intoxicated.

At the far end of the room near the dais, someone had set up a DJ station. Not very courtly, but Silver had ties to the Human world, and as Queen she could listen to any flavor of music her heart desired.

I broke away from Simone and the others and jogged toward the setup. The table had two turntables. A bucket tucked underneath the table was filled with ice, still in its frozen form, along with bottles of water and cans of energy drink.

The dais was decked out in red and white velvet ribbons, the seats of the wooden thrones covered with tea light candles in full flame. Shadows clung to the back corners. A pair of eyes shone in their depths.

A pair of terrified eyes.

I hopped onto the dais.

A trembling voice said my name. "Kevin Landon?"

Underneath the shaking, I recognized him. I stepped into the shadows with him, the warmth of the torchlight fading from my back, and hunkered down in front of him.

"Mr. Nance?"

His salt-and-pepper hair, normally slicked back and neat, stuck out in five directions, his skin pale. He wore a brown, pinstriped suit and tie with a tan button-down, but where it would normally be neatly pressed, it'd become a collection of wrinkles.

"What the hell are you doing here?" I asked.

"I have no idea. I went to sleep in my own bed and woke up here."

I'd have said that was impossible, but that word didn't have much meaning for me anymore. "When?"

"What do you mean? Last night," he said. "At least, I think it was last night. Is my daughter with you?"

I narrowed my eyes. He should've been able to see her. "She's here."

"Thank God. Please tell me she's all right."

"Mostly."

His relief was so thick, I could've held it in my two hands. He wasn't an innocent. He'd discovered everything he could about Simone and her new life. He knew about things most humans shouldn't. But he just wanted her back, didn't he? That was all he wanted.

He closed his eyes for a minute. When he opened them again, he said, "A girl. She came to the door. Selling cookies."

In August? Never happened in the history of the world as I knew it.

"She cast some kind of spell on me," he said.

"She said she'd give you what you were starving for?"

"Not in so many words."

She didn't have to say anything at all—she'd dropped me into that memory of my mother instantly. It'd been so real, it overwhelmed all my senses.

A set of feet hit the dais behind me, accompanied by the flutter of wings. Simone. "Kev?"

"Here," I said. "With your father."

She was at my side in the time it took for me to draw a breath. She knelt and leaned forward until she and Mr. Nance were nose to nose. "What did you do?"

"We were just establishing that," Nance said. He looked everywhere except at her.

"Establish it right the fuck now."

Her words struck him like a slap to the face. He looked at her then. "Do you hate me?"

"No. Do you hate me?" she asked. "Someone cut me with a blessed blade."

He blanched.

"So you know what a blessed blade is."

"Just so. I interrogated Mr. Davies."

He'd questioned Rude. Who would normally never divulge something like that.

Mr. Nance rubbed the bridge of his nose with his thumb and index finger. "He came to me, not the other way around. I told him I'd help him find you, Kevin. In return, he told me whatever I wanted to know."

I blinked at him.

"He was worried about you. Very worried. You were gone too long without sending word." He spoke to me, but he looked at Simone.

Evidently, telling someone you love that you can't be their daughter anymore didn't stop them from loving you. Or keeping tabs. Or worrying all to hell if you disappeared.

Simone's gaze softened.

"Rude knows where I am now. He knows I'm okay," I said.

Nance nodded. "Next time, you might consider informing us sooner."

Simone turned the conversation back to the knife. "Did you bless a blade for someone?"

"I don't want to talk about the girl with the cookies," he said.

Simone glanced at me. "What?"

"The girl who came to his door last night," I said.

Mr. Nance covered his face with his hands. "Please don't make me talk about her."

I leaned close to Simone. "Where are Malek and Beth?"

"Gone to search the rest of the place," she said. "Just to be sure, like we said."

I nodded. And extended a hand to her father. "Let's go, Mr. Nance."

He peered at me from between his fingers. "Where?"

"There's a chair over here. You should sit down."

"I can't sit there. That's for royalty."

Simone grabbed his arm and hauled him upright. "The Queen's not here right now. She won't mind."

He followed her to the closest chair—the former King's chair—and sat with a thud.

She bent over, resting her hands on her knees, wings pressed tightly together. "This girl—she was about ten years old, pigtails, dark blue dress with red polka dots?"

He took a shuddering breath. "She made me think you were at home in your room. There was music playing. You were singing. You were human. Thanksgiving dinner was nearly ready, and I'd be calling you down to eat any minute. Turkey with all the trimmings, mashed potatoes that were mostly butter, cranberries, and English peas. You wanted them that year. I could feel the heat waves flowing off the oven and the padded mitts on my hands and there were potatoes in my hair because the mixer had jumped in my hand and splattered them. The horizon outside the kitchen window was painted gold with the sunset. Brown leaves crackled on the grass when the wind blew and I could taste barbecue in the air. The neighbors were cooking theirs like that, outside. It was so real. I got lost in it."

Simone stared at him. "That was a good Thanksgiving."

He showed her a shaky smile. "When I picked up the knife to carve the bird, the little girl said I should say grace then and there, that I should bless the blade before it cut flesh. That would keep everything perfect. Everything would stay just the way it was and you would never go away. So I did it."

She took a deep breath and blew it out slowly. "And then?"

Mr. Nance's shoulders slumped. "She walked out the door and took my dream with her. I remembered everything, of course, and I felt so afraid that what I'd done would hurt you, Singer."

He never called her by her name, not since she'd begun the transformation from human to fae. She'd forbidden it, though she hadn't stripped it from his memory.

"I called Mr. Davies," he said. "I told him what happened. He poured me a double Scotch and tucked me into bed in my clothes, and I woke up here."

"He sent you here," Simone said.

Mr. Nance nodded. "Just so. At least it appears to have happened that way."

"Did Rude say anything to you about what he'd be doing while you were gone?" I asked.

"No, Mr. Landon, he did not. But his face spoke volumes. He turned colors."

"Colors?"

"Mostly red."

So, Rude was pissed. I'd known that already. He could handle himself, and he would. If he wanted to yell or punch me, he could do that later, if we lived through this mess.

For now, we had an empty Faery Court to contend with. Malek and Beth wouldn't find anyone. Simone had made that much clear.

"Mr. Nance, did you see anyone else after you arrived here? Anyone at all?" I asked.

He met my gaze. "There was a woman dressed like a knight."

A knight? "Sword, armor?"

"Not metal armor—black leather. She had spiky hair and rings in her eyebrows."

Silver. "Did she say anything to you?"

"'Tell them I've gone to close the hole in my realm. They'll know what to do.'"

"The hole in her realm?" Simone asked.

He nodded.

"There's a hole in Faery." She said it matter-of-factly, but with an *are you crazy?* lift at the end.

If there was a rip in one of the walls of the realm, it would leave Faery vulnerable to invaders, if anyone was of a bent to invade. After all, the realms butted up against each other—that much I knew. All you had to do was have a little magic, concentrate on where you wanted to go, and step sideways from one world to your destination, unless that place didn't want you to enter. Then, no matter how hard you tried, you'd never be able to find it.

If the realm was sick and vulnerable? That could be the perfect opportunity for someone as powerful as Famine.

All my thoughts about fate, about what Faery was, came rushing back. The havoc Famine could wreak here if she were able to take over, say, Silver's will—the thought made me want to throw up.

Silver had left the Court to protect the integrity of her realm and the safety of her people. If I were Famine, I'd have counted on that—on the Queen hitting the warpath and coming after me. I'd have counted on it so much, I'd have laid a trap.

I couldn't see any other way for it to go down. Famine had set the snare, and Silver would run headlong into it. Silver probably didn't remember who Famine was. What she was capable of. She wouldn't be expecting a Horseman of the Apocalypse, much less know what to do with one.

One other thing bothered me as much, if not more.

Silver had left the Court empty. She'd taken everyone with her, whoever was left to take. There was something else I couldn't put my finger on because I didn't know the lore. And I was human, so why should I? But I'd been given an office that meant something to Faery, so I had some feeling for the place and its strange rules. If I had to guess at what felt so wrong, it would be that something crucial to the realm was here in this hall. Silver had left it undefended.

She'd had to have known *that*. She'd have felt it, if nothing else. So, to leave like she'd done, she had to have felt as if she had no other choice.

There was something here that could not be left defenseless. I felt that as strongly as anything I'd ever felt.

"This is very bad," I said.

Simone's violet eyes darkened to black. "Get Malek."

# CHAPTER 7

MALEK AND BETH ran into the hall. Beth's footfalls echoed on the stone floor as they passed between the empty, decorated party tables. Malek, as always, was silent as a whisper. They took in Mr. Nance on the throne, gripping Simone's hands so tightly, her fingertips bleached white. Quiet tears streamed down his cheeks.

Malek raised a brow.

I shrugged. It wouldn't matter to him why Simone's father was here, just that he was. And that the man was a liability.

Beth was a little short of breath. "Got your text. What's the 911?"

"There's something here that's been left alone, but shouldn't have been. Famine will come after it." I could feel its name along the edges of my skin and on the tip of my tongue, but I couldn't speak it. "It's frustrating as hell. I think I can't tell you what it is because I'm not fae."

Simone narrowed her eyes. "I don't feel anything."

"I don't know why that is," I said. "I wish I did. I only know that I'm right. I feel it in my blood."

Malek signed. *Your blood?*

It whispered in my veins. No—it sang. It sang like Simone did when she wanted the feeling to penetrate to the core, only this felt more powerful. I'd never felt anything like it before. It was precious. It must be kept safe. Silver had left it. We couldn't let it fall into Famine's —or anyone else's—hands.

"I'm not being metaphorical," I said.

*Blood calls to blood,* Malek said.

I had no idea what that meant, only that I didn't like the sound of it, and that with Malek, it was always about blood. "Whatever. I just need you to believe me."

He gave me an appraising look. *I trust you. We set up our defenses. We guard it, whatever it is.*

"Not all of us," I said.

Beth cocked her head. "You want to split up. Where are you going?"

"The Singer and me." I glanced at Simone.

She met my gaze. "You want to follow Silver."

"She's walking into a trap."

"And we need her," Simone said.

I nodded. "I don't think we have much time. I think we should hurry."

"The question is, where is she?" Simone squeezed her father's hands and then let go, shaking the feeling back into her fingers.

Malek raised his hands. *When I work on someone, it ties me to them. To who they are. To what they are. It's not like the bond I have with Beth— it's something else—but it is a kind of bond. I can tell the Singer while you deal with her father. He should go back where he came from.*

Because telling me wouldn't do as much good. I might have some sense of Faery, and I might know some things I shouldn't, but I didn't know the realm like Simone did.

"I can't send Mr. Nance back to the Human world," I said. "I don't have the power anymore."

*Beth will take him.*

"Beth will totally not." She spun to face Malek. "I'm not leaving you. We've been over this a lot of times and it never ends well and I don't care whether you handled yourself for millions of years just fine without me, so don't even go there."

*I'm giving you an order.*

"Fuck your orders, boss."

Malek stared at her, but Beth didn't back down. She held her breath, unblinking.

He held her gaze for a long moment. The air around him seemed to vibrate. Then he sighed. *You'll watch him and swear to the Singer to keep him safe.*

"Fine." She took the steps to the dais two at a time. "Kevin, introduce us."

As she drew close, I could see that she was shaking—from fear or anger, or something else? I couldn't tell. All that mattered was that she had magic and that she would do what needed to be done.

I cleared my throat. "Mr. Nance?"

He wiped his eyes with the back of his hand and looked up at me.

I held out my hand for him to take. He let me help him up and walk him a few paces to the side.

"You understand what you need to do?" I asked.

He tried to smooth his hair back into its usual place, unsuccessfully. "I'm upset, Mr. Landon, but I'm not stupid. I'll try to stay out of the way, and failing that, I'll try not to die."

Simone moved to stand beside me and looked at her father. "I need to say something."

"You want privacy?" I asked.

She shook her head, gaze trained on Mr. Nance. "You keep trying to find a way into my life after I told you I didn't want you there. You keep reminding me of what I was when I was little. When I was fragile. When I had my whole life in front of me and the world was my oyster. You used to say that to me all the time."

"Just so."

"I'm not that girl anymore and I never will be again, no matter what you wish for. You'd be happy if I could pretend, but I can't."

He flinched. "You thought I'd prefer you dead."

"Would it be better to have me gone, so you could remember me the way you want and not be reminded that I can never be?" she asked.

"No," he said. No self-righteousness—just honesty.

She seemed to weigh choices. "I'm glad you're all right."

Tension rolled off of him in waves. With each passing moment, he grew taller, softer. "I'm glad you're all right, too. That's all I ever wanted."

"You don't want me back?"

"I do. But wanting and what is rarely intersect. You're not the girl you once were, and I'm not the man I used to be. If you're happy, then I can learn to be happy."

Simone's lips curved.

He answered her smile before turning my way. "Mr. Landon, why don't you introduce me to the serpent's apprentice?"

"You know who he is? Who Beth is?"

"I pay attention to what happens in my city, Mr. Landon. To my family. Their friends. Their associates. And what information I didn't already know, Mr. Davies supplied."

I could only wonder how he hadn't gotten into serious trouble sooner. I took him by the arm and steered him toward Beth.

She looked him up and down. "Don't be an asshole and we'll get along fine."

Mr. Nance offered his hand. "Same goes for you, young lady."

Simone descended to speak with Malek, whose bald head gleamed in the torchlight. For a second, I thought I could see his veins through his skin and the pulse of the blood pumping through them. Only for a second, then the vision faded. Like the new ability to hear Simone's heartbeat, I didn't understand it. I didn't want it.

*Wanting and what is rarely intersect.*

I didn't want Mr. Nance to be right, but I knew better. Possibly, I was losing my grip on reality. Possibly, there was something very wrong going on with the magic in this place. I'd been in this spot before, but this time felt different, as if I were perched on the edge of a cliff. Turn back, and everything would remain the same as it ever was. Jump, and everything would change.

I made my way toward Simone and Malek. "We know where we're going?"

She nodded.

Malek signed. *Don't fuck it up.*

I bristled, but bit my tongue when I realized he was teasing. I'd never seen him do that before—at least, he'd never been that way with me. "Hold down the fort."

Simone took me by the arm and led me a few feet away. "Silver's on the other side of the realm. We just happen to be in the one place in the whole realm that's connected to every piece of it by magic. There are roads from here to everywhere."

It sounded great, except for one thing. "Can people travel here on those roads, too?"

"That's the catch."

"So, when we open the way or whatever you're planning to do, we could be letting them in?"

"Yes. But Malek will take care of things here."

I'd have to trust that. I had no reason not to. This was my plan, for crying out loud.

Simone wrapped her hand around mine and spoke softly in my ear. "Hold on. If I lose you, I might never find you."

I squeezed her fingers.

One minute, we stood in the great hall. The next, stood at the nexus of the Faery roads. This was nothing like crossing into the In-Between, or moving between the Faery realm and the Human world I belonged in. There was no fire. There was only ice.

The nexus was a crossroads, but not the kind I typically thought of. Instead of two roads that intersected, there were three, plus one that seemed to begin in the center. That meant seven possible paths leading out from the nexus. All of them glowed bright blue, the same color as the hottest part of a candle flame. And the center of the crossroads itself rotated clockwise, slow and steady.

Waves of cold flowed from the paths. I could feel the chill through the soles of my sneakers. Everything around the roads—if there was anything—was hidden, wrapped in frozen darkness that felt slick on my skin. The whole of it, dark and bright, did something strange to my sense of direction, even my sense of up and down.

I felt no frame of reference. No context. We might as well have been floating in space, except no stars winked overhead. No moon. Just vast velvet night.

When I spoke, my breath fogged the air. "Which one do we take?"

Simone pointed with her free hand toward a path to our right. Or I thought it was to our right. The center of the crossroads moved as she gestured, so I couldn't be sure.

"Where does it lead?"

"To the Door of Death," she said.

Faery had its neighborhoods, its equivalents of cities, states, and nations. The Forest of Dreams. The First Forest. The Sunless Sea. I'd heard the names of these places a fair amount during my time as go-between, and more after I turned fae, but I'd never heard of the Door of Death.

"What's that?"

"What it sounds like."

The circle turned beneath our feet, carrying us with it. As it brought us around to the path Simone had pointed to, we jumped onto it. The road felt no more stable than the circle had, but unlike the circle, it felt sticky, holding fast to the soles of my feet. Lifting them felt like prying two magnets away from each other. We took seven difficult steps. On the seventh, the road fell away under us.

We dropped like stones through the chilled dark, onto a field of tall, thin grass.

Simone landed on her feet, her wings moving to steady her. I landed on my ass hard, a jolt of pain flashing through my tailbone that made me grunt and curse under my breath. I scrambled upright with the scent of crushed green in my nose and mouth and a rime of frost on my face that I felt when I lifted my hand to rub the bridge of my nose. I inhaled the perfume of fresh air with a faint hint of cow patties. The fragrance didn't do anything for my queasiness or my dizzy head.

The perpetual twilight of Faery cast shadows over the field, but the uncanny mood it created didn't hold a candle to the creepiness of the circle of giant granite stones that surrounded it.

The circle had to have been a hundred feet across, and the stones were too big for people to have carried, even fae people. They had to have been moved by crane or, given where we stood, by magic.

I caught sight of Famine from the corner of my eye. She crouched near the ground to our left, a body at her feet. No, not a body—I could see the rise and fall of her chest. More than that, I could feel her breathe, the stabbing pain in her lungs and the ragged draw of air. There was blood in her spiky silver hair.

Silver.

I heard two words inside my head. Silver's thoughts. *Stupid, Kevin.* Then she went silent.

I ran toward them without thinking, Simone calling out a warning behind me. I wanted to stop. I *tried.* But my legs refused to obey until my feet skidded to a halt directly in front of Silver and Famine. I fell to my knees beside the injured Queen of Faery.

Silver looked up, wild-eyed and ghost-pale and not seeing me.

I glared at Famine, who met my gaze. "What did you do to her?"

Might as well ask what Famine had done to me to draw me this close, what control she had over me. This was scarier than the magical anomalies. This was a total loss of control.

Famine reached out with her index finger and touched my brow with a spark that burned.

The earth began to shake, rattling the circle of stones. The stone to my right cracked in half from top to bottom with a sound like thunder. The two granite halves fell away from each other. Where they'd been stood my mother.

Not the dream of her. Not the memory of her. My actual mother.

Her messy brown hair streaked with summer gold. Her sunburned, freckled face. Her bare, sandy feet and cut-off denim shorts and long denim shirt worn over her purple tank top. The wind carried her scent. She smelled of salt and sweat and diavolo spaghetti sauce. She blinked her brown eyes and walked toward me, her feet bending the tall grass.

I tore my gaze away from her. She couldn't be real. She had to be a ghost. A summoned apparition. I turned toward Famine, but she and

Silver—and Simone—were gone. There was only the grass and the stones and my mother and me.

Mom came within a foot of me before she stopped walking. She studied my face.

"You're older," she said.

The sound of her voice knifed through my heart. A moan clawed its way up my throat. It took every ounce of will to swallow it. If I allowed myself to make that sound—if I heard myself make it—I'd break.

This was so much worse than being transported into a memory. This was real.

I spoke carefully. "How are you here?"

"This is where I came after that drunk man took me out of the world."

I'd been raised to believe in Heaven. But now I knew a lot more about the world—all the worlds. "If I ever saw you again, I figured you'd be wearing the dress we buried you in. The black one. And your pearls."

She shook her head. "I hated that dress. I loved the beach."

"That afternoon—making dinner together in the kitchen—it's my favorite memory."

Her face softened, her eyes filling with kindness. She looked at me with so much love. "Mine, too."

My voice shook. "Are you okay, Mom?"

"No, Kevin. You saw me before, when you were in the In-Between. You had a choice to stay there with me and you refused to take it. You thought to yourself that nothing could ever bring me back."

The vision of my mom in the kitchen was a trap, just like this was a trap, a poisonous gift. I didn't know what would happen to me if I chose to take it. Maybe it would kill me, or maybe it would just hold me in thrall, under a spell.

Did that matter? I couldn't believe my mom was standing there, almost close enough to touch.

For a second, I thought I heard singing. It sounded familiar, but I couldn't place the words or the voice.

My mother took a step toward me, then another. She raised her hands and cupped my cheeks. I breathed in her smell and looked into her eyes and my heart melted.

"You did what you were supposed to do," she said. "You grieved and you grew up and you became someone I could be proud of, Kevin. You thought about me and you missed me, but time dulled the pain. Time gave you a life beyond me."

That was the natural order of things: if not forgetting her, then forgetting the pain of losing her, or at least having it fade a little. I hadn't left her, though. She'd left me.

She spoke as if she'd read my thoughts. "I'm sorry."

"It wasn't your fault."

"Sorry all the same. But that's not why I'm here," she said. "I'm a distraction you can't afford. You're about to be changed forever. Your spirit is here, but your body is still with Famine and your friends. Famine will do something to you. No one will be able to stop her, and no one will be able to fix it. You need to wake up, Kevin. Can you do that for me?"

"Will I see you again?"

She didn't answer. Somehow that was worse than if she'd said no.

Instead she said, "Hurry back the way you came."

"How?" I asked.

"Your heart, Kevin. Follow your heart."

My heart was breaking. It would keep on breaking no matter what I did.

Either I could let my spirit go with my mom while Famine did something terrible to my body, or I could turn around and find my way out of this vision or whatever it was and do what I could for Silver and Simone and Malek and Beth. They were still living, as far as I knew. My mother was not. I couldn't help her, but I could help them.

I looked at my mother. Her eyes filled with unshed tears. A breeze blew from behind her, turning her gold-streaked hair into a wild wind of its own. I didn't want to say goodbye.

*Follow my heart.*

My heart was with my friends. One friend in particular.

I could hear Simone's heartbeat again. It was faint, but it was there, beating hard and fast, like a jackhammer. I closed my eyes. I reached toward the sound and fury.

Simone's voice was a whisper that became a shout. "Kev!"

I opened my eyes and stared into her violet ones. "What happened?"

She wrapped her hands around my shoulders and shook me. "Are you here? Are you in there?"

I grimaced at the lightning pain that tore through my healing wound. "Yes. I'm here. Where's Silver? Where's Famine?"

Simone loosened her grip. "Famine's gone. She disappeared. Silver's still here. Her mind is somewhere else, like yours was. And she's bleeding out."

"Did Famine do anything to me?"

Simone shook her head.

"Are you sure?" I asked.

"I think so," she said.

That would have to be good enough. I tried to get up.

Simone rolled me to my left. "Silver's right here."

The Queen lay flat on her back. A pool of blood spread from her back. There was a knife in her chest, buried to the hilt. From the position, it'd been driven straight into her heart. How she was still breathing? I didn't know everything about Faery anatomy or what it took to kill a Faery Queen. She was alive, and her eyes were open, but whatever she saw, it wasn't us.

I took her hand in mine. I called her name. She didn't respond. I listened as carefully as I could, so carefully I swore I could hear the grass grow underneath us. I couldn't hear Silver's thoughts. Wherever she was, there was definitely imminent mortal danger, but she wasn't broadcasting.

I glanced over my shoulder at Simone. "Do you have any magic you can use to get her back?"

Simone shook her head. "I tried singing to both of you while you were still out. It didn't work."

I'd heard it, the singing. I'd never seen Simone's voice fail to work when she put her will behind it. "Famine's too powerful?"

"I've never battled a Horseman of the Apocalypse before, Kev."

Simone couldn't wake Silver up. I had no powers to counteract the spell the Queen was under. I was just plain Kevin Landon, the guy with the important job that didn't mean anything anymore. Silver was done for and I couldn't do a damned thing to stop that.

Except follow her into her mind.

I'd done that only once, with the Faery King. But he'd been in my mind at the time, so I had a trail to follow. Here and now, I had no such thing and no hope of finding it on my own. But I wasn't on my own.

"Simone, you said you can't sing her awake," I said. "Can you sing me into her vision? Can you sing me to where she is?"

Simone sucked in a breath. "I don't know. It's still Famine's magic."

I nodded. "Designed to keep people in the traps she lays for them."

"But not out."

I prayed that was the deal. "Let's hope."

Simone rested her hand flat on my back. I felt it fever-hot through the fabric of my jacket and shirt. She took a deep breath and began to sing.

*Oscail do shúile.*
*Into Silver's stream*
*Into the river of dreams*
*Into the twilit wonder*
*Flash of light and roar of thunder...*

I heard nothing else. I didn't feel my body fall or my eyes close. I only smelled sulfur, so strong, so pervasive, that I could only have followed Silver into one place. The In-Between.

A one-room cabin in the In-Between. Two sleeping bags sat in one corner, rolled up and packed away. A milk crate served as a table, a whole lot of seven-day jar candles lit on top, the candles' flame jumping with disturbed air currents, throwing shadows on the dusty floor.

I knew this place. I'd been there. Famine had attacked me, and I'd caught my first glimpse of Silver.

She huddled in the far corner now, holding her head in her hands, eyes rimmed in smeared black kohl. "You're not supposed to be here."

"Neither are you," I said.

"I'm waiting for Max."

Her boyfriend, the one with the black feathers for hair. "You two got back together? You left him, right? When the King exiled you?"

She nodded. "You know why he exiled me?"

"Because you tried to take the sickness that's infected Faery onto yourself."

"And, in so doing, I doomed the entire realm. I fixed it, though. I found your friend Stacy, and she took me to Malek. What I asked for was so huge, and the price was high, too."

"What did you give up?"

"My memory."

My body and mind and soul—my whole being—rebelled at the thought. "No."

"I remember nothing from before the spell Stacy cast. Malek would've told you that?"

"Something like it."

"I only have what Max told me about what happened, about who I am. That, and what I've built since I came back to Faery."

"You're the Queen."

"Some job I'm doing in that department," she said.

I narrowed my eyes. "If you don't remember anything that happened before the cure, how do you know who I am?"

She blinked. "That is a very good question. I shouldn't. I mean, Max mentioned you when he told me the story of how I came to lose my memory, but he didn't give me any detailed description or show me a picture of you. You should be a stranger, but you're not."

"Or maybe it's because I'm the go-between and you're the Queen."

She shook her head. "It hasn't worked that way with anyone else. I know that much from watching my stepfather rule."

"Then what?" I asked.

She took her time answering. "I think it has to do with you. Something about you. And I think it's because I'm dying."

"There's a knife in your heart," I said.

"It's more than a knife."

Oh, shit. "A blessed blade?"

"How do you know about those?" she asked, then answered her own question. "Oh, because of Simone?"

I flinched as she spoke Simone's name. I wasn't used to anyone else using it. Then again, anyone else was usually human, and Silver was fae, and she was the Queen. She would know. "It happened to her. Famine tricked her father into blessing the knife."

She grimaced. "There's only one person in all the worlds that matters to me like that. Only one person who she could've gotten to do it."

"Max," I said.

"Max." She took a breath and blew it out slow. "Famine put me here. She trapped me here in this place. She set me to wait for Max, but he's not coming. She got him to bless the blade and then killed him. She thinks I don't know. I'm the Queen. I know what happens to everyone under my rule. I can't even grieve him. I don't have the luxury of time."

I couldn't wrap my heart around how terrible that was, how much it must hurt. "I'm so sorry."

"Thank you." She cocked her head. "How did you get here?"

"In your vision?"

"No," she said. "Here at the Door of Death."

"Simone brought us on the Faery Roads."

"No," she said again. "She shouldn't have done that."

"We wouldn't have gotten to you in time if she hadn't."

"Kevin, those roads stay open until you close them. Did Simone close them?"

I shook my head. "I don't think so. We came here and saw you and Famine. I ran to you and Simone followed."

That was what I'd feared. I'd said as much to Simone.

I held out my hand.

Silver took it. Her skin was cold, but her grip was strong and full of electric charge. It passed from her hand into mine, racing up my arm and into my chest. For a heartbeat, I couldn't breathe. The world of Silver's vision went still. Even the dust motes in the air froze in time. Then all at once, the world sped up and Silver's fingers squeezed mine.

"Follow me out," she said.

I stared at her. "I thought I'd be doing the leading."

"I've got this. Your turn will come soon enough."

I didn't understand what she meant, but I understood the part about getting the hell out of here. Faster than I could blink, I felt a change in the air. The absence of dust and the cooling breeze. The tall, thin grass I knelt on and the crushed green scent of it. Simone's hand was warm against my back. I looked down at Silver. Her eyes were not just open, but bright with pain.

Simone spoke low. "Kev, I need to get to her."

I crawled out of the way, blades of grass sticking to my palms.

Simone knelt where I'd been. "I need to pull this out."

"It won't matter in the end," Silver said. Tears streamed from the corners of her eyes, wetting her cheeks and her hair.

Simone frowned. "I was afraid of that. But it will still be better out than in."

I looked from her to Silver and back again. "How will you stop the bleeding? She's hit in the heart."

"She's the Queen," Simone said. "She can command the people and the land—the whole realm. Her body is part of Faery. She can command the bleeding to stop."

I'd never known the King well enough to get that kind of information from him. What it meant to be the ruler of the realm. The power it gave him.

"Then she can heal herself," I said.

Simone shook her head. "It's more complicated than that."

I didn't understand. "How?"

"She has more important things to worry about than herself."

It wasn't that I didn't know that, only that I didn't factor it in. It was so alien to my experience as a human being. I was one person. An individual. Sure, my choices affected other humans, but it wasn't the same.

That kind of power Silver wielded was woven in to who she'd become. But it wasn't just about the power. It was the responsibility that came from it. If Silver could command all of Faery and everyone in it, including the land, then that made her responsible for all of her people. For the whole realm. If everything went smoothly, and all she had to worry about was the occasional small dispute, no problem. If things went like they had for the past year, that was a different story.

When she'd been the King's stepdaughter and only heir and tried to fix everything wrong with Faery in one fell swoop, it'd backfired horribly. And the King had exiled her as punishment because the backfire could've—would've—ended the entire realm. The important thing about that had nothing to do with Silver, at least not in terms of the big picture. Silver had not only almost killed herself, she'd almost killed everyone and everything she'd ever loved. An entire race of people. An entire land.

To undo her terrible mistake, she'd given up her memory. From the first time she'd gazed into her mother's eyes until her last kiss, she'd traded away everything she'd ever known to save Faery.

Now that she wore the crown, the stakes were that much higher. Her lover was dead. Murdered. There was no one left to fix her mistakes, to tell her it would be all right, or to send her away. She had to do it all herself. She had to make the right choices or all of Faery would pay the consequences.

I met Silver's gaze. She took in the look that had to have been on my face. I could never hide my feelings well.

"You understand," she said.

I nodded. "As much as I can."

"It takes practice."

I never wanted that kind of practice. I didn't see how I could avoid it, not with an impending apocalypse. I might not have much in the way of magic, but I knew things, knew people. I'd probably end up dead sooner than I wanted to be, but I'd never walk away if I could make the smallest difference.

"Silver, can you command the poison from the blade not to kill you?" I asked. "Can you clean it from your blood?"

She took a shuddering breath. "The blade struck me through the heart. With any other fae, that wound would've been fatal. Even with the power I have, the poison has spread through my body. It's tainted every cell. There's so much of it. As Queen, I could do what you say, but it would take weeks. I would be unconscious for all that time. Do you understand that?"

It'd taken Simone one night to heal the poison in her system, but that blade had only pricked her skin. It hadn't pierced any organs. The poison had damaged her, but not like with the Queen. Not so completely. And that wasn't even the point.

To have a hope in hell of healing herself, the Queen would need to check out at the moment her people and the realm itself needed her more than ever. If she chose herself over Faery, Faery would die. And, because Faery fed magic to all the other worlds, the rest of them would follow.

"What do you need?" I asked. "What can I do?"

Silver looked from me to Simone. A wordless communication seemed to pass between them. Simone shook her head.

Silver grabbed Simone's hand, the one wrapped around the hilt of the knife in Silver's heart. She squeezed hard enough for her knuckles to bleach white. "I need you," she said. "Both of you."

Simone's voice shook. "I can only promise for myself."

Silver softened her grip. "That's good enough for me. Now pull this damned thing out of me."

Simone blinked back tears. "Kev, I need you to be ready. When I pull out the knife, press your hand to the wound."

Like I would with any other. I started to shrug out of my jacket, intending to use it stanch the wound as best I could.

"No," Simone said.

"But with just my hand—"

"It'll be enough, Kev. Trust me."

She didn't give me time to think about it. She wrapped her free hand around the hilt, lacing her fingers together, and pulled with everything she had in her. The blade slipped free with a sickening, wet pop, followed by a geyser of thick, red blood.

I reached to clap my hand on top of the wound. My hand passed too close to the blade in Simone's grasp. The tip of it sliced open the heel of my palm as if my skin were made of butter. I winced, fighting the instinctive urge to pull back my hand. There was no time. I pressed it against the heart wound in Silver's chest, fighting the torrent of red, ready for the gusher to continue pumping through the cracks between my fingers. Instead, the rush of blood slowed.

"That's the best I can do," Silver said. Her eyes were open and clear and filled with determination. She hadn't for one second lost consciousness or wavered. "Help me up, Kevin."

"Are you sure?" I asked. "If I take my hand off the wound, will it be all right?"

"As all right as it'll ever be."

I pulled my palm away. Moving it should've hurt, but it didn't—not at all. The cut the blade had made was already knitted.

"What the—"

Silver interrupted. "Help me, Kevin."

I pushed to my feet and offered her both hands. She let me help her up. She was heavier than she looked.

Simone stepped up beside us. She folded the blade closed, swiping at the blood on the casing, and slipped it into her back pocket. I opened my mouth to crack wise about her aim with the knife, but the look on her face stopped me cold.

Compared to me, she was a high-level expert at keeping her feelings to herself. But in that moment, she looked haunted.

"Hold on to me," she said. "Eyes and ears open."

Silver slid an arm around Simone's waist, and I did the same.

"Don't let go, Kev."

"I won't."

No matter what had happened between us, no matter whether my humanity or her fae-ness kept us apart, she'd never lose me. I wouldn't allow it to happen. No matter how hard the odds became, I wouldn't give up.

It was that complicated and that simple.

We'd never talked about having a life together because we'd never thought we could have one. Better to keep the hurt locked inside. Don't even dream of acknowledging your feelings, and even more important, never say the words out loud, not to each other. Because once the words were spoken, they could never be taken back. And that would only make it hurt worse, like some horrible self-fulfilling prophecy of pain.

In all likelihood, the Queen would die and take the realm and everything else with her. Even if she stopped whatever Famine was trying to do, even if she kicked the Horsewoman out of Faery and lived, Silver would be so weakened she might sleep for a lot more than a week. She might sleep forever, like a fairy-tale princess.

It was also probable that Simone or I would die helping Silver defend Faery, or defending the people we cared about who were back at the Court. Much as Beth annoyed the crap out of me and Malek freaked out the primal part of me that knew he was the world's most contradictory super-villain, I cared about them. I cared about Mr. Nance, too. He'd been a pain in the ass, but also an ally when I'd needed one most. It didn't matter to me that Simone had a hard time with him. The man was her father.

If I had to die to save Simone? I'd do it in a heartbeat. She'd do the same for me.

So where did that leave us?

It'd be better if Silver weren't here to hear. On the other hand, Silver seemed suddenly to look everywhere except at Simone or me, as if she knew what I was about to do.

"Simone," I said.

She turned her head to meet my gaze.

I made my voice strong and clear. "I love you."

A ten-ton weight lifted effortlessly off my shoulders, warmth wrapping around my heart. I waited for her to say something.

Instead, she stared at me. "Say it again."

"I love you," I said.

She searched my face. After a moment, she seemed to accept what she saw there. "I love you, too."

"Let's go," I said.

Silver nodded. "Now."

Simone spoke a word too softly for me to hear. The Faery road appeared in front of us, wreathed in blue fire.

# CHAPTER 8

THE COURT REEKED of blood. A thin film of red slicked the floor in front of the dais, splattering the oak steps and the edge of the platform. I breathed and tasted the coppery stench. My stomach twisted on itself.

Except for the horror of so much blood, the great hall looked the same as we'd left it. Pristine and ready for the party that'd never happened. Torches burned in their sconces along the walls. The overshadowed scent of the flowers that seemed less smothering and more sickeningly sweet now.

The room was empty. No people. No monsters.

For a heartbeat, I thought I heard the echo of Beth's voice, faint and filled with surprise, calling for Malek. I shook my head to clear it. The echo faded.

I glanced at Silver. Her skin was several shades paler than it'd been in the field. She stared at the mess on the floor.

Her nostrils flared. "This is human blood."

She could identify the species of the bleeder by its scent. Disturbing, but not as disturbing as the question that struck fear in me.

Whose was it?

Malek didn't qualify as a member of the species. Neither did

Famine. That left Beth. Or Mr. Nance. I glanced at Simone, who spun slowly around, taking in the gore. She stiffened.

"He has to be okay," she said.

I nodded. "Beth will protect him. She promised."

"It was stupid to let him stay here. I was stupid. I should've sent him home."

Where he'd have been vulnerable again. "There weren't any good choices."

She shook her head. "There's no trail."

Not a single footprint leading away, as if the person all of this blood belonged to had teleported out or simply disappeared.

"There's more," Silver said. "More blood. Some spilled in the antechambers—the rooms in back of the hall. Malek and Famine and one human are in the room behind that one."

I stared at her. "How—"

"This is my home. I'm as tied to it as I am my body. I feel what it feels."

Talking about the Court as if it were alive. Being so connected to it that she could pinpoint the location of those inside like I could pinpoint the location of a mosquito feasting on my leg. Damn.

"One human. Where's the other one?"

"I don't know, Kevin."

"But you can tell where Malek and Famine are."

Simone fisted her hands at her sides. "Silver can't answer the question because they're only human."

"It's not like you make it sound. They just don't register that way to my senses."

It wasn't that she didn't care. There were limits to her abilities, governed by what she was. "We have to get to them."

"There are more important things," Silver said.

"The thing you left unguarded."

She met my gaze. "That's impossible. You shouldn't know that."

"Everything's impossible."

She shook her head. The shaking sent a tremor through her whole body.

Simone turned to stare at Silver, eye to eye. "We don't have time for you to freak out right now. Tell us what you're hiding here so we can help you protect it. Tell us so we can get moving."

Silver looked past Simone to me. Fear sparked in her eyes, then faded just as quickly. She squared her shoulders. "If it's the will of the realm that you should know, then so be it."

"You're talking about the land as if it's alive," I said. "Just like you talked about this place."

"That's because it is—all of it. It has an intelligence of its own. And a heart."

A long time ago, Rude had taken me to the heart of Houston, the heart of the city, to make magic. It had been alive. It'd had a mind of its own. It wasn't a stretch to consider Faery in the same way. "The heart of the whole realm is here."

"It speaks to you."

Not with a voice. Not even with thoughts. "It's all emotion. Like I can feel what it wants me to feel."

She mulled that for a minute. "Then it's settled."

"What is?" I asked.

She took a deep, painful breath. "Go after Malek and Beth."

"And my father," Simone said.

"Him, too," Silver said. "Do what you can to keep them safe. Do what you can to distract Famine."

"And what are you going to do?" I asked.

"Take my throne. It'll connect me to the heart, lend me strength when the Horsewoman comes to face me."

Famine would definitely come for Silver. She was after that throne. She wanted Faery for herself.

"Can you take her on alone?"

"I won't be alone. You're here."

Against Famine, we were nothing.

Silver answered my thought as if I'd spoken it aloud. "You're stronger than you think."

Everything that had happened proved exactly the opposite. I opened my mouth to say so, but then snapped it shut when Silver looked at me the way the King used to—piercing any kind of front or mask I wore, drilling down into my deepest thoughts and feelings. It felt like a violation, as if I'd been stripped naked in a crowded room under a spotlight with nowhere to hide. Silver seemed to grow taller, the boundaries of her body stretching.

She was enormous, her wiry muscle more emphasized. Her feet no longer looked like plain feet—they'd grown roots that burrowed into the floor, punching their way through the floor and whatever foundation anchored the building, into the land itself. I harbored no illusions that they'd stick if she tried to lift them—just the opposite. Any step she took, the whole realm took with her. When she moved, all of Faery moved in her orbit.

Silver was the definition of power and strength. I might as well have been an ant. An insignificant ant under the spotlight of a magnifying glass in the sun.

The spotlight faded as fast as it'd sparked to life, though some of its heat remained behind. My skin flushed. Sweat beaded in my scalp and traced pathways down my cheeks and the back of my neck. Silver looked like a regular person again, as much as a Faery Queen could be a regular person. Whatever she'd seen in me, she kept to herself.

"Go this way." She took a step back, clearing the path toward the oak door behind the dais, its silver handle gleaming.

Simone slipped past her, taking the steps up to the platform two at a time, boots striking hard enough to shake the structure and rattle the ribbons. I dogged her heels as she ran past the thrones and hit the door with her shoulder. It shuddered in its frame and snapped open. We barreled through into the pale-lit antechamber.

There were torches in the sconces on the oak walls every few feet, just like in the great hall, but this room was the size of my living room at home, long and narrow and comfortable. Unlike my living room, no furniture graced the space. The brush of our steps on the floor, the same stone as in the great hall, vied with the shaky sounds of our breath.

Simone swung an arm in front of me, splaying her fingers against my chest. "Kev."

I followed her gaze. The floor cradled a single, still body, facedown in a pool of blood. Black hoodie, skinny jeans, brand-new black motorcycle boots.

Beth.

Her snake's nest of hair was more red than brown; her hands stretched out in front of her, as if she'd tried to break a fall. Her steel-gray glasses had tumbled off her face. They lay two feet to her right, one lens cracked. Her messenger bag sat next to them, the embroidered letters of her name slashed through. Whatever blade had done that, it hadn't penetrated the bag itself.

I knelt next to Beth, the blood soaking through my jeans. I reached out to touch her shoulder, realizing as my fingers got closer that her chest was rising and falling. Faintly, but that was all that mattered.

"She's alive."

"My father—"

Simone couldn't stay here. She needed to go after him. She needed to be sure he lived and breathed, to protect him.

She met my gaze, then glanced at the door that led to the next room and back again. All the things that remained unsaid between us —the things she wanted to tell me—flashed in her eyes. I thought I knew what they were. I hoped I did, at least. She spread her wings wide. They were a part of who and what she was. They were beautiful and strong.

"Go," I said. "I'm right behind you."

"You'd better be." She folded her wings tight against her back, ran for the door, and barreled through. It slammed shut behind her.

She wouldn't have taken the time to do that. Someone else had done it.

My heart thudded in my chest. Fear pooled in my gut, cold as ice.

I rolled Beth over carefully. Purple and black bruises bloomed around her eyes. Her nose had a new crook in it. Blood ran from her nostrils over the bow of her lips and the shelf of her chin. Tears salted her cheeks. Unconscious or not, they continued to flow.

I grabbed her shoulders with my hands and shook her gently. "Wake up."

Her eyes fluttered open. She blinked at me, then her eyes widened, words rushing out faster and faster. "What are you doing here Famine's here and she's after the Queen please God tell me you didn't bring the Queen back with you?"

"Slow down."

"No slower," she said. She tried to push up on her elbows, but couldn't seem to make her arms work. She clattered back down on the stone, smacking the back of her head. She hitched in two breaths and tried again, angling her chin at the door Simone had just gone through. "Malek's in there. With Famine."

"And the Singer," I said.

"Bad." She squinched up her face and winced at the pain. "Famine will hurt her."

Like she had before, through the sick fae girl. "The Singer's ready for that."

"No," Beth said. "Not like you think. You go."

"But you—"

Beth interrupted. "Fine."

"—almost died," I said. She might still.

She answered my thoughts rather than my words. "Malek will bring me back."

I didn't like the sound of that or the implications. Clearly, Beth felt differently.

She pleaded with her voice and her bruised eyes. "You go, goddamnit."

I slip-slid to my feet, bloody jeans sticking to my skin, and went for the door, pulling the knife from my pocket and flipping it open. Chances were I'd never get close enough to use it, but if I could be the distraction we needed to get the jump on Famine, I'd do whatever needed to be done.

I wrapped my fingers around the door handle and pushed. The door swung open. Darkness reached out and swallowed me whole. I couldn't see. I couldn't smell anything except salt and sand and diavolo spaghetti sauce. From the afternoon in the kitchen with my mom, the one I'd been thrown smack in the middle of the last time I'd seen Famine.

The part of me that'd frozen the night of the accident that killed my mother, the part that remained fourteen, wanted nothing more than to go back there.

The rest of me refused. That part won, hands down. Famine wouldn't get me this time. She had nothing I wanted. Nothing I was so hungry for that it would trap me.

The darkness dispersed like fog under the punishing scrutiny of the sun. In its place, I expected to see a room like the one where I'd left Beth. I expected to see Simone and Malek and Nance and Famine. Instead, I got the punishing scrutiny of the midday summer sun on browned grass and on live oaks whose branches stretched in long, curved arcs above the ground, shading only the earth beneath them, leaves singing in the breeze. A big, fat crow sat with its talons wrapped around the lowest branch of the closest oak, not a foot from me.

It looked me in the eye. *You shouldn't be here.*

I'd been so sure Famine couldn't take me. As soon as I thought that, the memory of Famine disappeared like so much smoke drifting into the clear, blue sky.

I blinked at the crow. It looked like the same one I'd seen in the Faery wood and the same as the one I'd seen in the In-Between. Either it was stalking me, or it was like some kind of guide. The crow only seemed to show up right before something bad. Like hearing thoughts during deadly danger, the crow was an omen.

All the hair on my body stood straight up. My mind stuttered for a second before I could think an answer at the bird.

*Where's here?*

As soon as I asked, I knew the answer.

When my friends and I had fought the demon, some of us had come here to gather an ingredient for a spell. Our city had been transformed from the vibrant, sprawling, bustling city into a dangerously magical, apocalyptic hellhole, and we were helping to fix that. We'd come to gather water from the heart of Buffalo Bayou, the heart's blood of Houston.

Amy had gone into the water to get what we needed. She'd turned into some kind of mermaid. She'd handed us what we'd needed to do the magic that would save the city. But she'd refused to come out. No amount of arguing made her change her mind. We'd moved on, and she'd stayed.

The sun sat low in the west, flooding the clouds with orange and gold light, gilding the leaves of the oak and the wings of the crow. The air was thick enough to cut with a knife and tasted of Gulf brine. The humidity raised a thin film of sweat on me and made my shirt and jeans stick to my skin. My jacket hung on me like a ten-ton weight. I stripped it off and let it fall into the newly mowed, sunburned grass without a second thought. A breeze gusted, rustling the leaves of the oak and the crow's feathers, lifting the hair from the base of my skull.

The skyscrapers downtown loomed ahead in burnished stretches of steel and glass and concrete, the glare of the sun off them so strong I narrowed my eyes to a squint. Thirty yards to my right, the parkway wound past, short oaks hugging the esplanade, fancy apartment buildings on the other side. The road should've been filled with cars and trucks and motorcycles and crazy bicyclists in expensive clothes with expensive gear taking their lives into their hands to mix it up with the vehicles. The road was empty, as was the jogging path that matched its serpentine curves. No walkers, runners, or dogs on leashes, tongues lolling in the heat.

Six feet to my left the ground rose to a low crest, then sloped down to the bayou. The grass had been cut to within a foot of the water's edge, where it grew tall and unfettered and dotted with dandelions. The murky water caught the reflection of steel and glass and concrete, soaking up the hum of toads and cicadas.

Amy.

Her voice carried from the water's edge, acknowledging my presence but not calling me over. "Kevin."

I gave the crow a last glance, then started toward Amy, wanted or not. I glimpsed her as I crested the small rise and started down toward the brownish-blue water, the current moving slow and steady toward the concrete and glass canyons, always reaching for the Gulf of Mexico. The top of her head, her hair blue-tinted black, sank under the surface. For a second, I thought she'd swum away.

I hadn't seen her in almost a year—a long time for a girl who'd been my every-day someone. She'd changed so much physically, magically. How else had living in the water, away from other humans, made her different? Could I even say I knew her anymore?

She broke the surface a few feet back from the edge, the water rippling around her shoulders. So, she hadn't run away, but she'd backed up, maybe not wanting to be that close.

She narrowed her eyes, meaning to fix me with a glare or just fighting the brightness of the sun—hard to say. Her face was pale as the moon that would rise later tonight, her shoulders covered in soft-looking moss that shimmered with water droplets. I looked for the motion of her arms, treading water, but didn't see it. Maybe she didn't need to use them. Maybe she had a tail that did the work for her.

Did she have magic? Would she use it on me?

Her voice had a muddy quality to it that hadn't been there before. She answered my unspoken thought. "You're under a spell."

What did that mean, under a spell? There was somewhere I was supposed to be, something I was supposed to be doing. It flitted at the edges of my mind. It frustrated like a word hanging on the tip of my tongue that I couldn't quite spit out. I worried at it for a moment, but couldn't hold on to the concern. It drifted away.

All my focus homed on Amy again. She'd spoken words as if responding to something I'd said. But I hadn't said anything out loud. "Reading my mind?"

"I wouldn't want to even if I could."

A low blow, but nothing I didn't deserve. "That's fair."

She shook her head. Water droplets flew from her hair. "Nothing about this is fair."

I took a shaky breath. "I'm not here to hurt you."

"You couldn't if you tried."

I had no idea what a mermaid could do, but I'd be a fool not to think it was plenty more than I could. That covered the physical. Emotionally, though? I'd already hurt her plenty without meaning to. I'd loved her, but I'd fallen in love with Simone, too, and I couldn't help how I felt. I'd made my choice between them by holding on to Simone, by keeping her in my life and in my heart.

That kind of thing happened between people all the time. I hadn't expected it to happen with me, but expectations didn't always match reality. I'd been an asshole. And Amy needed something from me I couldn't give her. No matter how much love I showed her, she didn't love herself. I couldn't fill an empty well.

She knew it. I knew it. That didn't make it hurt any less, and I didn't think her new form made her any less vulnerable to that hurt.

In that moment, the fleeting thought I'd had about what to remember, what to do, returned. I was under a spell, Amy had said.

"Why don't you tell me why I'm here?" I asked.

She shrugged. "How should I know?"

Famine. Famine had done this.

"You met any Biblical powers masquerading as little girls lately?"

She raised a brow. "You want to unpack that for me, Kevin?"

"There's a Horsewoman of the Apocalypse running around. Her name's Famine. She looks like a little girl—pigtails, glasses, Mary Janes. She's dangerous as hell, and she seems to be in the habit of talking people into hurting the ones they love."

Amy bit her lip. "You actually think I love you?"

"I still love you," I said.

"That makes you a fool, Kevin."

I nodded to give her the point. "Or just honest."

"Fuck your honesty," she said. "You never could be honest when we were together."

"I never meant to hurt you, but it doesn't matter anymore, does it?"

She sighed. "It didn't matter then. We weren't meant to be. The Singer was always there."

I'd worried about hurting Amy. I hadn't thought she'd wound me. I wasn't the one whose boyfriend was in love with someone else. Amy had called me a fool. She was right.

"It's not her fault," I said.

"You say. I should be able to blame somebody."

"Blame me."

"I do."

"Good. So what now?" I asked.

She studied me. "You said a Horsewoman of the Apocalypse?"

I nodded.

"For crying out loud." It didn't come across as angry. Amy sounded like what she had been—not only my girlfriend, but a valuable member of our anti-apocalypse team. The camaraderie surprised me. "What the hell are we into now, Kevin?"

*We.* I had no right to *we.*

I raised my hands. "I didn't know Famine even existed, for real, until yesterday."

"How'd you find out?"

"She attacked me. Beth filled in the details later."

"The nosy parker who helped what's-her-face summon that Demon? The one who almost got us all killed? Who almost destroyed the world?"

"Yeah, her. She's apprenticed to Malek now."

Amy rolled her eyes. It was a very un-mermaid-like gesture. "Figures."

There was something about Malek I needed to remember. Something about Beth, too. An image flashed in my mind: Beth's face, only without her glasses. Her skin, smeared with red.

"I think you should go," Amy said. "You can come back later if you live."

"If I live?"

"You know, if you live through what Famine's doing to you right now."

"I don't know."

"Yes, you do, Kevin. It's happening right now. You walked through that big oak door with the wooden handle. You were going after Malek and the Singer. The Horsewoman is in there, too. Remember?"

Beth's face and the blood. Her broken nose. She was barely breathing. She'd said if she died, Malek would bring her back. I should leave her and go help him. Help Simone.

Silver was dying, too. The dying Queen of Faery waited on her throne for Famine to attack. She needed our help to have a chance to live at all. No, not to live. To save her people. The land. The realm. The heart of Faery.

I held Amy's gaze. "Why am I here?"

"Because Famine dropped by my rock on the bayou and offered me a chance at payback for what you did to me because you fell in love with the Singer. She said she'd make you come back here and explain. She said I could keep you as long as I wanted, if I wanted, and if I didn't, I could kill you."

My jaw dropped.

"Why are you surprised?" Amy asked.

"You'd never do something like that."

"No, Kevin. The old me wouldn't have. I'm not her anymore."

"Then why are you telling me this?"

"Because you can't explain what happened any more than I can. And as pissed at you as I am, I don't want to kill you. You're someone I used to—someone I love. I can't stop feeling that or anything else. And I'm pissed at you for that, too. I'm made of feelings, one-hundred percent feelings. I only kill my dinner because I have to eat. Even if I wanted to kill you, you're not really here. Your consciousness is, but your body's not. Your body is in Faery. Famine lied to me."

Every word hit me like a punch to the gut.

"You have to get out, Kevin."

"Then let me go."

"I already have," she said. "You have to let me go."

The guilt I felt, the wishful thinking that things had been different, the need to talk to her like we were doing right now, hoping I could somehow make things right between us. I couldn't tie it off because you couldn't put a tourniquet around feelings and cut off the circulation. Heartbreak wasn't that kind of wound.

We both had unfinished business with each other. It would never *be* finished. It would only be one more thing that couldn't be fixed. We'd have to live with it.

If we lived.

Behind me, the scrape of talons on bark and the rush of wings catching air announced that the crow had taken off. It circled overhead, its shadow flowing over me like water. It circled once and called out. The caw echoed inside my head.

The crow's shadow winged away to the west. The breeze rattled the branches of the oak for a moment, then the sound vanished. I glanced over my shoulder. The tree had disappeared, too. And the sun-browned grass. And the glass and steel towers of downtown.

Last of all, the tall grass and dandelions and the brackish water of the bayou faded, and Amy along with them.

She raised a hand to wave. There were webs between her fingers.

She turned to mist in front of me. Her voice shone in the diamond-droplet particles that hung in the air. I heard it not with my ears, but with my heart.

"Try not to die, Kevin."

I blinked. The mist enveloped me. It filled my nose and mouth and shoved itself down my throat. I coughed until my lungs threatened to come up, heaving air, trying to breathe. In a flash, the mist dissipated. In that flash, I saw the shiny silver edge of a blade slash for my throat.

I didn't have time raise my arm in defense or to duck. I twisted away from the arc of the knife and did the only thing I could—I fell backwards, keenly aware of the wooden door and wall behind me, unsure how close. I landed hard on my left arm with my wrist trapped under my body. I heard the snap of bone before bright pain screamed through my arm. My head whipped with the momentum of my fall and smacked against the stone floor. The world fuzzed for a long second. Then it snapped back into color and motion, everything too bright and too sharp.

The blade whiffed through the air above. The Mary-Jane-clad feet of Famine planted on the floor in front of me seemed larger than anything that should belong to a little girl. Famine's feet looked like small boats. And her legs could've been tree trunks. I drew back both legs and kicked her shin. She didn't even flinch.

"Kevin Landon," she said.

I looked up. She had to have been fifteen feet tall, her dark eyes enormous behind the lenses of her tortoiseshell glasses, her blond pigtails like small, furry animals hanging from either side of her head. The red polka dots on her dress looked saucer-sized.

She held my knife in her right hand. She'd taken it from me and I hadn't put up any kind of fight. How could I when she had me trapped inside a world of her making?

"She didn't go through with it," Famine said. Meaning Amy. Amy hadn't killed me.

It almost hadn't mattered. If I hadn't come to when I did—if Amy hadn't snapped me out of my dream—Famine would've cut my throat.

"She's not the only one who missed," I said.

I tried to roll to my right, to use my right hand and arm to help me stand—or crawl. My arm or my wrist was broken. I had no weapon.

Famine raised a huge foot and brought it down fast and hard. I moved my leg just in time. Her shoe smashed down where my knee had been. The force of the blow cracked the stone.

I rolled fast, fueled by enough adrenaline to get a knee under me and gauge the distance to the wall at two feet and change. I lunged for it, using it to scramble upright. I dodged before I heard the knife cut the air. The blade whizzed past my ear and buried itself halfway to the hilt in the wood of the wall.

Where was Simone? Where was Malek? And Mr. Nance?

I spun to look past the giant Famine and caught glimpses of furniture—a brown leather chair, a sofa that appeared to be covered with moss, a tree stump that served as a coffee table. A pair of black wings framed a large, oval mirror that hung on the long wall across from me. Real feathers, real wings, really belonged to an actual bird. Or maybe an angel. Or another fae. Torn from their body and hung up like a trophy.

Mr. Nance sat with his back against the wall underneath the

wings, head lolling to one side. Was he trapped in one of Famine's hells, or just unconscious? No way to tell. No time, either.

Malek stood in the far corner. His face was slack and his eyes faraway. His hands hung at his sides, fingertips twitching.

I yelled his name.

He didn't move. No, wait—he took a half-step forward as if he were walking through water.

"Malek!" I yelled again.

Famine backhanded me with stunning force. If the wall hadn't been there to hang on to, I'd have gone down in a heap. The moss sofa and the tree-stump table blurred. I saw two of everything instead of one. Including Famine's hands wrapped around the hilt of the knife, yanking it from the wall in a hail of splinters.

"I wanted to possess you," Famine said to me.

"I'm not that easy." A bluff, because I had been. She'd trapped me repeatedly. She was stronger than I could ever be.

"You're already chosen. Already marked,' she said. "I was too late to get a hook into you."

I shook my head. "The fuck are you talking about?"

She tightened her grip on the knife.

Behind her, Malek moved—this time, not just his leg, but his whole body. He launched himself at Famine's back.

She saw his threat reflected on my face, but not in time to do anything about it. She narrowed her focus. If she could kill me before Malek reached her, she would.

Her arms arced over her head, fingers laced around the knife's hilt. Malek grabbed hold of the blade and Famine's hands and used her own momentum to force her off-balance, slamming her to the ground. The knife flew from her hands, the blade embedding itself in the chair's back with a thump. Malek stomped a booted foot on Famine's chest and left it there.

She struggled to push it off, to get up, but she couldn't budge him. Her great size didn't matter at all against him. She opened her mouth, teeth bared. She lunged at his leg, ready to bite—then stopped at the last second.

She'd forgotten for a minute who he was. What he was.

"Kevin," he said, "bring me the knife."

I pushed away from the wall, tripping over my feet, cradling my left arm in my right. There were two of Malek and two of Famine and—

"Where's the Singer?"

Famine spoke through clenched teeth. "I took her down. I—"

Malek pressed his boot harder into the Horsewoman's chest, cutting off whatever she'd been about to say. "The knife, Kevin."

I stumbled past them. Famine reached for my ankle. I smashed her fingers with my heel.

I sank to the floor behind the leather chair, the grain unnaturally large and unlike any leather I'd ever seen. The tip of the blade had pierced it and stuck in the stuffing. I narrowed my eyes. In a moment of clarity, I realized that what I'd assumed to be batting was flesh and blood. Living flesh and blood.

Everything in the room was alive. The room itself was alive.

It took all the strength I had to pull the knife free. It made a sound coming loose that I never wanted to hear again for the rest of my life, a sound that reminded me of the scream I'd let fly when my bone broke. It made me want to throw up.

I handed off the knife to Malek. Instead of using it to stab Famine through the heart or the eye or wherever he could reach, he sliced open his own arm. His poison blood dripped onto Famine's dress. Where it touched, it sizzled.

And it was on the blade now. Anyone stabbed with that blade who wasn't Malek or Beth would die in agony.

If Famine were too powerful for Malek's blood to kill her, it would hurt her. It had to, didn't it? Judging from the way she looked at the knife now—calculating, but not cold, because she carried a touch of fear in her eyes now—it would do her some damage. Bad damage. She wouldn't take that risk.

We had her.

That meant Silver was safe. She'd have time to heal. It meant Simone was safe, if she was still alive.

Famine had taken her down. What did that mean?

I searched for Simone in the shadowed corners of the room and found her in the space behind where Malek had been trapped in the dream Famine had made for him. She laid on the stone, curled into the fetal position, hands protecting the back of her neck. Scratches had torn the skin of her forearms. She'd put up a fight. Blocked sharp fingernails, and from the looks of the scratches, teeth. Famine's bite.

Simone was breathing, thank God. And trembling. Shaking so hard her teeth rattled. She looked at me with one rolling, violet eye, like an animal bracing before the slaughter. She blinked. Her gaze cleared.

"Kev?"

I knelt beside her and pulled her close with my good arm, trembling with her. "Tell me you're all right."

She cupped my chin in her palm. "You're not."

"I'll be okay. I'm gonna need a cast, though."

"Where's—"

I answered the question before she could finish asking. "Malek has Famine. We're out of the woods."

She shook her head. "We've never been out of the woods, Kev. There's no way we captured Famine that easy."

"You call that easy?"

"Scratches and broken bones? Yes."

When she put it like that, I couldn't argue. I wanted to believe. I'd fought my way out of Famine's trap with Amy's help. I'd nearly had my throat slit. I had at least one broken bone and probably a concussion to match Beth's. If Malek hadn't snapped out of his dream when he did, I'd be a tenderized, pulverized, bloody mess on the floor, bleeding out.

I glanced over my shoulder at Malek. He met my gaze with his ancient eyes a heartbeat before he sailed into the wall, slamming his back and his head and plummeting in a heap to the stone.

Famine, who had somehow thrown him, rose to her feet in one fluid movement, the knife she'd ripped from Malek's hand clenched in her fist. She opened her hand, balancing the hilt on her palm for an instant. She popped it into the air and grasped it with her fingertips and launched it in a silver flash at me.

I couldn't move out of the way this time. Not with Simone in my arms. I had seconds. The knife would slide into me. It would pierce some vital organ. My lungs. My heart. Malek's blood, still on the blade, would enter my bloodstream like a curse. I'd die screaming, like the others Malek had killed.

I pushed Simone away from me in case I misjudged Famine's aim. It was all I could do.

Simone moved—but not away. Not to safety.

She was fae grace to my solid, human clay. Liquid fire to my earth. She couldn't move fast enough to shield me completely, but she could get in front of the knife. The blade buried itself in her arm, slicing through flesh and sinew like butter, the tip catching on bone.

Malek's blood entered her body and, with it, his poison. I couldn't see her face. I couldn't see it in her eyes. But I felt it in the slowing of her heartbeat. In the lightning pain that seized and held her heart prisoner. I felt the torture begin, the rending of every cell into bloody pieces, before she drew a shocked breath. The bloodcurdling terror that clawed its way up her throat and into her mouth.

Simone screamed.

# CHAPTER 9

SIMONE'S ANGUISH stabbed through to the core of me, paralyzing and blinding. She crumpled three feet away, writhing. *So close.* I reached for her with my good arm, but I couldn't touch her. I couldn't help her. I couldn't even comfort her as she died.

I braced my back against the oak wall behind me, cornered like an animal. I tried to rise, but a chill swept through the soles of my sneakers, spiking along my spine. It felt like death, coming hard and fast.

Famine barreled toward me, a predator sure of the kill. She was on me faster than I could stand. Faster than I could get a leg out front to trip her or slide out of the way.

She wrapped her fingers around my throat, lifting me off the ground high enough that the toes of my shoes barely brushed the stone. I couldn't breathe. I couldn't speak. Pressure built inside my head with nowhere to go.

I clawed at Famine's grip with my good hand, trying to peel away even one of her fingers. I couldn't get any traction. All I could see were Simone's wings creeping open, strong and fragile and transparent over the feathers of her peacock top, her back arched and mouth open in agony. Malek struggled at the foot of the far wall, arms shaking and sweat dripping from his forehead as he heaved himself upright. All of it—all of them—black and white and fuzzy, the images fading in and out.

The huge lenses of Famine's tortoiseshell glasses reflected my bulging eyes and beet-red skin. She grinned, not from enjoyment, but with determination.

"If I can't make you do my will, you can't be allowed to survive," she said. "You're marked and you don't even know it. You're marked for the sacrifice."

Sacrifice? Was that what she was doing to me now?

Whatever Malek could do to help, it wouldn't be in time.

I heard a voice call my name. Not his. Not Simone's. Not Famine's.

The voice held the authority of a Queen. Silver.

*Hold on, Kevin. I'm coming.*

Famine showed no sign of having heard. Neither did Malek. Silver had spoken only to me—or had I imagined it?

I was the one who heard thoughts, voices echoing in my head on the brink of mortal danger. That was my magic. I had to trust it. I had to trust the Queen.

Had Silver gathered enough strength to have half a chance of defeating Famine—or at least a shot at holding her own? Could it be enough? I didn't see how. With the wound Famine had dealt her, Silver didn't have much life left. She was the one who should hold on. I should go to her. But I couldn't. Because I was dying, too.

Famine hadn't gone after Silver. From the moment I entered the room, Famine had focused on me. There were far more powerful people in this room. People who could cause her far more trouble than I ever could. People who qualified as actual enemies, who could square off against her and matter in apocalyptic times.

Why me?

Famine tightened her grip. The gray in my vision darkened. The pain of my arm receded. I couldn't feel my legs. Simone had stopped screaming. Whatever remained of my heart shattered into a million pieces.

I tried to hold on to consciousness. Because Silver was coming. I had no idea what she could do other than sacrifice herself—and her whole world—to take out Famine. But not to save me. I was the distraction. Someone to hold Famine's attention so she wouldn't see Silver bearing down on her until too late. An honorable way to die.

I could no longer see Famine or Malek. I couldn't see Simone's body. I couldn't see the door to the room. I trusted my ears to hear it open when Silver came through. Then I could let go. I held on to that with everything I had.

Every second felt like an eternity. I counted each one as if the next meant salvation.

But the door didn't open. It took precious moments—the final, tripping heartbeats before I passed out—before I understood that it never would. Not from the outside.

Something else was happening.

I didn't hear Silver come, but I felt her—the spotlight, the sun's light shining on me, hot on my face and filling my eyes. Suddenly, I could see. My vision cleared and then did something better. It pierced the mask that Famine wore, her little-girl costume grown large. Behind the glamour, Famine was a bottomless pit.

An empty hole that sucked everything into it, and that everything went nowhere at all and filled nothing. A hunger that could never be sated. Even when the world finally died and nothing remained but the stars, Famine would still be this thing. She'd outlive us all, and she'd never know what it meant to be filled, what it meant to be at peace, what it meant to be loved.

Silver's light took hold of my body, penetrating my skin, slicing into my flesh and blood and bone, unmasking whatever I could hide, everything I'd never wanted another person to see: my insecurities, my fears, my broken heart:

How I could never have been enough to stop my father from drowning himself in alcohol or going after the Faery King. The way I almost hadn't been enough to rescue him. I could never have done it without my friends' help. Dad appreciated it, but some part of him still wanted to get lost and never be found, and I didn't think that part of him would ever go away.

The fact that although I was willing to die, I was terrified of dying right here and right now. Mostly I was terrified of not being there to help my friends when they needed it, even if I could never be more than the third spear-carrier on the left, or the guy who cooked spaghetti for dinner while we hashed out magical threats, or whatever other nameless, faceless, thankless role needed me to fill it. I wanted to see them again. I wanted to at least say goodbye.

Simone. Simone had died saving me. She'd suffered a death I wouldn't wish on my worst enemy. I hadn't been able to lift a goddamn finger to save her. Would I find her on the other side? Would she wait for me? I thought she might.

We could be together then. It would be all right.

My mouth opened. Words flowed out. They were not my words, not spoken from my heart or mind, but they rang in my voice.

"You've lost," I said. Not my words—Silver's.

Famine flinched, but she didn't loosen her grip. "You can't have him. He's mine. He's almost gone."

"*Almost* is nothing," I said. "*Almost* is no fire. *Almost* is only smoke."

I seemed to grow taller, the boundaries of my body stretching until my feet touched flat on the ground, solid and unwavering. My neck grew larger—wider, more muscular—and Famine's grasp faltered. I pushed her away—the heel of my hand struck her solar plexus. She grunted and staggered back.

I glanced down. My feet in their sneakers no longer looked like feet—they'd grown roots that burrowed into the floor, punching their way through the stone and into the land itself.

I more than saw it. I felt it. Tendrils burrowed through the soles of my shoes into the stone, obliterating everything in their track, surging into rich, dark soil underneath. The roots kept going, soaking up moisture and nutrients—the blood of the land—digging down past long-buried stones and bones, deeper into layers of earth that had never seen the surface, spiraling down into pulsing, spinning, molten iron. The core of Faery. The core of the Earth.

The heart of Faery was also the heart of all the worlds.

I touched it. More, I could tap into it.

Any step I might take, the whole realm would take with me. When

I moved, all of Faery would move in my orbit. I was power and strength. Famine might as well have been an ant. An insignificant ant under the spotlight of a magnifying glass in the sun.

Holy ever-loving Jesus H. Christ in a sidecar. The fuck was going on?

Silver's voice rang inside my mind.

*Kevin, listen. I don't have long. There are things you need to know. You asked if I could take Famine on my own. The answer's no, Kevin. I didn't have enough power in me. Even if I'd not been mortally wounded, it wouldn't have mattered. I am only fae, even if I am the Queen. No Fae being could keep a creature like Famine out of the realm. Not alone.*

I hadn't thought my heart could race any faster, but I'd been wrong.

*You think you're nobody. Do you know how rare it is to be an ambassador between species? Between human and fae? It's not just a title. You weren't just appointed because you happened to be in the right—or wrong—place at the right time. You have something inside you that marks you as kin to us. Your magic.*

My magic made me a freak. But it also helped people, saved lives.

*It makes you strong, Kevin. It's about connection. You have a connection to all other humans when they're at their most vulnerable. That makes you powerful. You've never chosen to use that power to hurt others. You've put life and your heart and your soul on the line for the ones you love. That makes you a good man. A good human. You're the only one here who has half a chance to take the choice I'm about to offer and make something good come from it.*

*What choice?* I asked.

But I already knew. If Silver was dying—and she was—there was no one designated as her heir. No one to take over the throne, to keep Faery alive. No one.

I couldn't see her at all. I could hear the bittersweetness in her voice. The hope and the sadness in it.

*Like I said, Kevin, no pure fae can keep Famine out of the realm.*

And no human could do it either. But together, we had a fighting chance. That was what she meant. That was what she wanted. What

Faery needed. She was asking me to give up my humanity. To become something different, new.

*No, Kevin. I'm asking you to become something ancient, something not seen in any world for millennia.*

*If I say no?*

*Then Faery will change,* she said.

*You mean it will die.*

*Maybe. It will surely no longer be what it is and has always been.*

Famine would shape the realm in her own image. Now that I'd seen her true form, could I allow that to happen if I had a chance to prevent it?

I had a life. I had goals and dreams and, despite the magic that had hijacked my life, I still wanted those things. To go to school. To find out what I might be like if I had a chance to go away, to choose whom and what I wanted to be. I had every reason to say no.

If I said yes, I'd be chained to Faery for as long as I lived—which, given what I understood about the fae, would be for centuries, for millennia—if not forever.

There was no time to sleep on it. To weigh pros and cons, to talk to Rude or my dad or even Malek, to consider the consequences. It was now or never.

Even if I had the time, it came down to the fact that, if Faery fell, all the other worlds would follow. Fighting for all those worlds, all those people—that was a battle worth everything. Saving the worlds was worth dying for. Saving the heart of all the worlds. Guarding that treasure. Using it on the side of right. Even if it meant all the hard choices and responsibilities, and giving up the future I wanted.

I couldn't say no. I wouldn't.

*What will happen to me?* I asked.

*You'll have my knowledge, my power. You'll have human knowledge and power, too. You'll know what to do.*

*Will you be in my mind like you are now?*

*Yes.*

Just one word, but it meant I wouldn't be alone.

*It'll be a hard road, Kevin.*

When had my road ever been easy?

I accepted all of it. I was who I was, no matter the power that would flow through me. Simone had said as much. I believed in her. I trusted her.

I drew a deep breath through my aching throat. *Whatever you need to do, Silver, do it.*

The shining that enveloped me grew brighter—so bright I had to close my eyes. It didn't help. The shining filled me up inside, too.

My senses sharpened to a razor edge. I tasted blood and poison and bile. Smelled the dry scales of a serpent's skin, the tannins in the oak beams, the rime of water and decay in the stone. I felt the urgent rage and sucking emptiness inside Famine and the endless depths of sorrow in my own heart, the trickle of sweat running down the back of my neck, funneling between my shoulder blades.

As if gazing into a mirror, I saw myself as I'd always been. Just Kevin. The rush of my blood filled my ears. The sound of my heartbeat.

Time slowed to a crawl. In a flash, it stopped.

My human senses shattered like glass, shards exploding out like a thousand mirrored blades. The pieces of the shattered mirror traveled in an instant to the far reaches of Faery—the Forest of Dreams, the Door of Death, the Faery Roads—and all the places I'd not yet seen but that now belonged to me. Were now part of me.

In an instant, the shards and the reflections in their mirrored shine rushed back into me. They sliced me open, embedding themselves in my bones. In my heart. In my blood. In every cell, and in every memory within those cells. My body gathered them in, absorbed them —healed around them—and the broken bone in my arm mended itself in a flash of heat.

I fell to my knees, the shock of striking the stone floor shuddering through me. I registered the pain, but I didn't feel it. My Kevin-self, my Kevin-ness, embraced a companion. Silver's memories, her consciousness, her essential self, wove into mine. For a moment, I could see the seams in the weaving, the borders and boundaries of who was who, and which was which. And then the boundaries, the borders, melted into each other, and there were no seams at all. No separation.

One whole being. One brand new being.

I blinked in slow motion, closing my eyes on everything I'd known. I was no longer just Kevin. Silver was no longer just Silver. There was no longer a distinct sense of *I*, only *we*.

My senses merged with Silver's. I heard all the things I would normally hear. And: I heard the brush of Famine's dress against her legs and the small pops in the joint of her elbow as she pushed herself off the floor. I heard, too, the swing of her pigtails as they disrupted the air and the folding of her fingers to make the fist she intended to hit me with.

I opened my eyes. I saw the punch rush toward my nose. I leaned left, out of the way. Her fist raced past my face, all the force in her body contained in the momentum of her arm. She was off balance. I pushed her, like I'd done a minute ago—this time in the direction of her punch. She went down like a bundle of sticks, limbs tumbling over each other.

I didn't hold with the possibility that I'd become some kind of badass fighter all of the sudden—I was just faster. I noticed more. It gave me a better shot in a fight than I'd ever had.

As much as I wanted to pummel Famine, to beat her down until there was nothing except that gaping black hole left of her, all that would get me was my ass handed to me. It'd be a waste of what Silver had given me. I had one thing to do and one thing only. I stood and turned to face Famine.

She scrambled to her feet. Before she could lay a finger on me, I wrapped mine around her neck and held on while she struggled. She flailed her arms. Tried to kick me—and connected hard. I'd be lucky if the bruises didn't go bone-deep. But I didn't let go.

Her skin felt sticky and hollow. Because, unlike me, she didn't need a fully functioning throat made of delicate parts and plenty of breath to speak, she had no trouble getting words out. "I don't know what the Queen told you, but you can't do anything to me. I'm beyond you, Kevin."

"We can clearly see under the circumstances you're not."

"We?" Famine asked.

I cocked my head in Malek's direction as he made his way toward us. "We."

Famine narrowed her eyes. "But Silver—"

"When you said I was marked for the sacrifice and didn't even realize it, I thought you meant I was the sacrifice," I said.

"Silver gave up her life," Famine said. "But so have you."

Famine wasn't wrong. I'd lay bets she didn't know how right she was. "We'll see how it goes from here. Or I will, but you won't."

"You can't kill me," she spat.

"Not yet. But I can send you away."

And I could do one other thing. I slid a fingernail across the thin skin of her throat. Blood welled into the curve of my nail—at least it looked like blood. I considered it, and I considered how to throw her out of Faery for good.

I didn't need to march her to the edge of the realm and open a gate to make it happen. I *was* the whole of the realm, the center and the edge. I tightened my grip around her throat. I opened my mouth and spoke words from Silver's memory in a language not my own. I heard them in that tongue, dripping with the raw power of fae and human magic, echoing against the wood and stone. I understood them in my own language.

*You are banished. I forbid you from entering this realm forever on pain of death.*

Although I didn't have the power to kill her myself, those words did, should she trespass in Faery ever again. They bound her in ways that went beyond the physical. If Famine had a soul—if a being like her could have a soul—the binding went as deep as that.

As the echo of the last words faded, so did Famine. She vanished in a flash of light. She would not return.

Malek laid a hand between my shoulder blades. It felt cool, solid, steadying.

I glanced over my shoulder. For someone who'd been trapped in a nightmare and thrown across the room, he didn't look even a little worse for wear.

He lifted his hands to sign. I turned away. I didn't need to see what he said. Not yet.

There was something else that needed doing first. Something I demanded. I was the King of Faery. I was the land and its people. I could harm. And I could heal.

I looked at Simone. I hadn't been able to do that much since she fell, screaming. I thought she'd died alone, but she hadn't. Mr. Nance held her to his chest as if she were a sleeping child. Maybe to him, she was. He'd lost his suit jacket and his tie. His hair stuck out in every direction. Blood smeared his wrinkled shirt and pants. Tears ran in fat drops down his cheeks.

The blood had come from Simone. It'd streamed from her nose and her mouth. And, God, her eyes. Her purple and black mane was soaked with it. Her wings, crumpled. Her fingertips, raw—she'd clawed at the stone.

I hunkered down beside her father and held out my arms. "Give her to me."

He shook his head.

Malek loomed over Mr. Nance, signing quickly. *Would you really rather have her dead than alive and out of your reach?*

"What did he say?" Mr. Nance asked.

I translated.

Nance stared. "Is it possible to make her live?"

I nodded.

He transferred her into my arms. She felt light. Flesh and blood remained, but her soul had flown. Her soul, which was part of this place. Part of the land. Part of me.

I brushed the damp hair from her forehead and laid my brow against hers, whispering words in the language I didn't quite know. I heard the rustle of tiny wings, the first beat of Simone's heart. I pressed my lips to hers, tasting coppery blood and patchouli and her first indrawn breath.

# CHAPTER 10

I WAITED FOR SIMONE to regain consciousness, to open her eyes, to look at me. I needed her to be okay. I needed her.

The hard stone under my knees felt unforgiving. Torchlight created shadows all around us. Sticky copper overpowered every other scent in the air. I took a deep breath, willing Simone to do the same.

"What's wrong?" her father asked.

"I don't know."

He narrowed his eyes. "Kevin—"

I heard my name, but everything he said afterwards faded. I gazed at Simone—*into* her—looking for damage I hadn't expected, for any reason she could still be in trouble. Had I underestimated my ability to heal? Malek's blood was deadly, and he was older than time. There were so many things I didn't yet know, or couldn't possibly know. Raw panic rose in my belly. I shoved it down.

It wouldn't help Simone. She was all that mattered.

Instinct, and Silver, spoke whispered in my mind. I couldn't make out the words or their meaning, only the emotion that fueled them.

*Nothing had gone wrong. Simone was fine.*

So why hadn't she come back to me?

I pressed my forehead to hers, taking no comfort in the contact. Her body was here and healed and well, but the part of her that made her essentially herself was...gone. I closed my eyes, searching the corridors of her mind, taking unexpected turns and hitting dead-ends, shining a light in every darkness.

Nothing.

I called her name, the sound of it echoing inside her skin, skimming the surface of her bones, tremoring through her veins all the way to her heart.

No answer.

I inhaled a shaky breath and tasted a hint of patchouli. The only thing I'd smelled the first time we'd met, in the big yellow school bus in the alley downtown. A steady beat—her heartbeat—raised the hairs on my arms and the back of my neck. Her heart shone with a light I'd never seen before, not like this. Silver and gold and scented with roses, and, underneath he gilt and richness, a force greater than what I'd felt when the Queen had become part of me. I had only one word for it, the only one that made sense, that felt right.

Magic.

In the space of a breath, I slid into the magic—Simone's magic—not understanding where I was, because, even after everything I'd seen and felt, this should've been impossible. To be inside her magic. To be inside her heart.

I didn't see blood, or feel the contraction or expansion of muscle. I saw twinkling lights along the open windows of the bus, the torn green vinyl seats stacked deep with oil paintings. I breathed in smoke flavored with earth and spice, and caught the wink of the full-length mirror in the back, a blink of light against glass amid the explosion of tie-dyed fabrics.

A second ago, the rubber-treaded aisle had been empty, but no longer.

Simone stood there in her peacock halter and leather pants, wings wide behind her, violet eyes wide and focused on me. In her hands was the white cloth packet tied with red string, the one she'd carried in her pack. The one she'd had since childhood. The one that had been so important to her.

"Why are you here?" she asked.

I cocked my head. "I followed you. You remember what happened?"

She thought for a moment. "Did I die?"

"Yes." It was the worst word in the world, the worst feeling. But it was over now, wasn't it?

"You brought me back."

I nodded.

"Then why am I here?" she asked.

That was for her to answer, not me. This was her choice.

*Her choice.*

There was a question I didn't want to ask her, but needed to—because she hadn't been born fae, and because right here and now with Silver's and my power fresh and wild, there were no limits to what I could heal for her.

"Do you want to come back with me? To Faery?"

She furrowed her brow. "What else would I do?"

"You told me you miss your human life. You miss being human."

She glanced at the cloth packet, fingers worrying at its edges. She caught me looking, and she knew why—I hadn't asked her what was inside, and she hadn't told me. I could guess that it held human things. Things she hadn't wanted to let go. Things she shouldn't have to.

I'd never heard Simone talk about her mom. What happened to her. What she was like. Maybe she kept reminders of her mom in there.

Maybe I was wrong. Maybe it didn't matter. The secrets it held belonged to her. It was her choice to keep them or not.

She took a deep breath and exhaled shakily. "You want me to give up my magic? To be human again?"

I raised a hand to block the sound of the words, then forced myself to lower it again. "It's not about what I want."

She took a tentative step toward me. "You can do that for me?"

The word caught in my throat. "Yes."

"And you would do it if I asked."

Not a question this time, but a statement of fact. I would do anything for her. "Yes."

She closed her eyes, fingers tightening on the cloth. "It's a generous offer, but I don't think I'll take it."

I stared. "Are you sure?"

A moment later, she looked at me, her gaze full of wonder. "And I'm not going to change my mind down the road."

"You sound so sure. How can you be?"

"I love you," she said. "I want you to know that, and also to know it's not why I'm staying."

She loved me. She'd showed me in a hundred ways. Still, I wasn't the reason she wanted to remain in Faery, to remain fae. "I don't understand."

"It's not about you, Kev. You're enough—more than enough. But I'm staying because I want to. Because magic is part of me now. And because this world—this beautiful place that influences every other world—is broken. I can help mend it."

That, I got. But it wasn't that simple. "This beautiful place took everything you had. It pulled you out of your old life and gave you a new one without asking. It ruined everything."

She shook her head. "The King did that, Kev."

"I'm the King now." I couldn't bear the thought that she might think of me the way she thought of him. That I would remind her of what he did.

"You're not him, Kev. You're you. And that makes all the difference. Not only because I love you, but because I trust you."

Hearing her say the words broke something in me. It felt hard to stand. I willed myself to remain upright. To move forward from this moment. I hoped like hell to be worthy of her love and trust.

She closed the distance between us, sliding her arms around my waist, meeting my gaze with those wondrous eyes. "How do we get home from here?"

How did we get here in the first place? By not just listening, but hearing each other. By not just looking, but seeing the truth in front of us.

"Oscail do shúile," I said. *Open your eyes.*

One second, we stood in the bus's aisle. The next, I knelt on the stone floor of the antechamber, Simone in my arms. She met my gaze. I'd never seen anything so beautiful.

Beth's voice shattered the moment. "Damn, Kevin."

Beth's voice. Which meant Beth was all right.

I turned to see her fidgeting in Malek's arms, deep circles underneath her eyes. Her clothes were bloody, but she didn't appear to be in any pain—not physically, anyway. "Good to see you."

"I died," she said.

I sucked in a breath. Malek had brought her back, and he looked like he'd gone to hell and back to do it. The circles under his eyes were deeper, his skin so pale, I could see blood vessels beneath it. He also looked as if he'd kill anyone who got within a foot of Beth, friendship notwithstanding.

I glanced back at Simone, who'd met her father's gaze.

Mr. Nance swallowed hard. "You're not coming back with me."

She shook her head.

His voice shook. "I'd give anything to have you back, but I won't take what you love or who you are from you. You have to decide, and, no matter what you choose, I'll love you."

"I love you, too. And I'm staying here, but I promise not to be a stranger."

His eyes welled with tears. He blinked them away. "I'd like that."

She looked at me. "All right?"

It was more than all right.

We had a lot to sort out, and we would do it together. For now, there was unfinished business.

Parts of the realm would be in chaos. There was no telling how much damage Famine had done, and no way to find out except to check everything and everyone with a freakin' magical microscope. The people here might not be too keen on having a partially human

King, either. They would deal, best-case scenario. Worst case, I'd have insurrections and rebellions to put down.

On top of whatever I faced, there would be more people whom Famine had spelled to come after me—fae, or human, or Order assassin. They'd have to be hunted down. I'd do everything in my power to heal them. Failing that, they'd have to be killed. If it came to that, I'd be the one to do the killing, with my own hands and magic. They were my responsibility now.

I hated that thought. I hated that it came as naturally as breathing.

Silver had at least been raised to understand royalty. To become royalty. I'd been raised to keep my nose clean and study hard. I had a lot to learn.

I met Simone's gaze. "How long do you figure we've got until the hordes descend?"

"Until morning, at least."

Tomorrow. What day was it? What time? I freaked out for half a minute before I realized that I knew those things now like I knew my name. Outside, the full moon had risen, shining its pale light on the land. It was midnight. Time held its breath for a heartbeat, then moved forward into the new day.

Malek raised a brow.

"What?" I asked.

"He's got advice for you," Beth said.

I waited, expecting him to set her down so he could sign. Instead, she spoke for him.

"Tell them the truth. All of it. Hell, call a meeting. All the Faery brass. Tell them what Silver did and show them what she left you. They'll believe you. You need them on your side."

"What she left me isn't exactly visible," I said.

She laughed. "That's what you think. Why don't you see for yourself? Check your back."

I wasn't sure I wanted to know what I'd find. "I have something for you before you take off."

Beth grinned. "Famine's blood."

I nodded.

Malek set her down then, carefully, and pulled a handkerchief from the back pocket of his pants. I used it to mop the congealed red from under my nail and gave it back to him.

"Think you could do something with that? I don't know—some kind of magic that will keep you two safe from her?" I asked.

Malek smiled. If he weren't my friend, the sight would've chilled me to the core. Because he was my friend, it made me feel marginally better about our chances.

He walked out with Beth. If I wanted to, I could sense their exit from the Court, into the woods and out of Faery. But I needed to look in the mirror.

Simone and her father came with me to the mirror on the wall. I turned toward the glass to take a look at my back.

Where the skin had been a blank canvas before, one of Malek's magical tattoos took up all the real estate. It was a big silver mirror, like something out of a fairy tale, and not just body art. It was an actual mirror. The real thing.

"Silver did this," I said. "Why?"

Simone cocked her head. "Why don't you ask her?"

Ask her. Because her consciousness—her soul—lived inside mine.

Silver had commissioned the mirror to make herself into a reflection of truth for her people. She knew who she was. The people would know who they were. All of them, on straight-up terms, equal footing. No games. No ends that justified the means.

It was a good way to begin. The best place to start.

"Did you know?" I asked Simone.

"About the ink?"

I shook my head. "About what Silver planned to do with me. I heard you two, back in the field where you pulled the knife out of her heart. You said you could only promise for yourself."

"That I would see things through. That I would help her in whatever way I could," Simone said. "Even if that meant that I died, or came away changed."

"She didn't tell you what she had in mind?"

"You know she didn't."

Because I had Silver's memories. I could tap into her consciousness. Her love of her people and her realm, and her hollow grief over her partner. Something else to get used to. I nodded. "I need to get through the day. I'm gonna need you by my side. Can you do that?"

"I wouldn't miss it." She twined her fingers with mine and squeezed. "Dad and I will hold down the fort—if you'll stay for a little while?"

"Just so," he said.

She held my gaze and looked at me the same way she always had—not as a newly minted freak or as the most powerful being in Faery. "Come back to me, Kev."

No matter how much I'd changed—and it would take me months to figure out how much—to Simone, I'd always be Kevin. She loved me for who I'd always been. I hoped she would love me for who I would become. I trusted that. I trusted her. For now, we had each other.

# CHAPTER 11

I SAT IN THE GRASS at the edge of the bayou as the sun sank below the horizon of the Human world, turning the surface of the water to burnished gold and copper. The bayou ran high, and the current moved crazy fast—a tropical storm had blown through town and dumped a foot of rain in thirty-six hours. Although I'd lived most of my life in Houston and understood the thrashing wind and crashing waves and rising floodwaters, I felt the aftermath now like never before. The world had been washed clean. Given a second chance. There was nothing gentle about it.

My pants were tight and bound in places that made me fidget, brown leather where I preferred denim. A white linen shirt with laces where I'd expect buttons had replaced my favorite T-shirts. I wore brown leather boots instead of sneakers. It felt like a costume. Either I'd get used to it or I'd have to raid the mall before I went back to Faery.

One thing I didn't expect to ever get used to: the itch between my shoulder blades. The tips of white feathers had poked through the skin there, just outside the edges of the mirror tattoo. I'd have wings again, sooner rather than later. No longer a memory, but a reality.

Memories were precious. I held onto mine as tightly as I could, especially since I understood so deeply now what Silver had given up when she'd sacrificed her memory to save her world.

I could feel Silver inside my head, her thoughts like ripples across still water—something else to understand and explore in the days to come. I'd need her wisdom and her strength. We all would if we hoped to survive.

Mosquitos hummed as they hovered at my ears, but they didn't bite. My blood no longer satisfied them. A light breeze rimmed with brine kicked up from the southeast, rustling the leaves of the oaks. In the tall branches of the closest tree, a crow stood sentry, reporting on the goings-on in the park in a constant stream of thought-talk that played like a radio announcement in the back of my brain: cars and trucks and a river of cyclists on the parkway, joggers with dogs and a murder of humans riding Segways on the footpath that hugged the curves of the road. In the parking lot, a bunch of empty vehicles and one old, occupied Chevy Suburban.

My best friend in the entire world sat in the driver's seat of that Chevy. Rude wore an orange Hawaiian shirt that matched the color of his buzz cut, along with a pair of khaki cargo shorts and scuffed sneakers without socks. He ran the air conditioning on high and the sound system on deafening. Metallica. With him, it always was and always would be.

I'd sent him a message through fae channels. He'd met me at the gate in the great oak outside of the pub in the Montrose. I'd stepped through into the human world as someone subject to his jurisdiction. He was a faery seer, magical law enforcement in the Human world.

The air had smelled of spent rain, spilled beer, crushed green, and car exhaust. He'd smelled of bubble gum and cigarette smoke and the heady spice of magic. He'd taken one look at me and said his favorite word: *Dude*. Then he'd wrapped me in the biggest bear hug I'd ever been suffocated in.

I used to think I saw him when I looked at him. His too-school-for-cool vibe, his extraordinary luck, how he tried to hide the way his parents ignored him. When I looked at him now, he glowed—his eyes, his breath and his hands and the tattoo of the city that spanned his entire back—those shone like the stars on a cloudless night, even through the kaleidoscope of his damned shirt.

If I wanted to, I could've told him his future, his fate, as it stood at the moment. I didn't want to. I'd only wanted to hug him back and be happy about it. For his part, he held off asking me questions and drove me here to see Amy one last time.

I would've waited for hours for her if I needed to. I had a lot more patience than I'd ever had before. It didn't take much imagination to figure the cause might be that the fae lived forever. If you had forever, then time took on a different meaning.

A moment later, the moving surface of the water broke into a cascade of ripples as Amy's head and shoulders emerged into the night air. She swam towards me. I expected her to stop at least an arm's length away, but she kept coming, reaching out to grab hold of the bank. The moss that covered her skin looked like velvet in the gloaming.

"You didn't die," she said.

My lips curved. "Not the usual way."

"No." She studied me. "I don't know whether it suits you, though. The change."

"Doesn't matter," I said. "I didn't have a choice."

She shook her head. "Of course you did, Kevin."

"You know what I mean."

She inclined her head, giving me the point. I was who I was. I couldn't have made a different choice and lived with myself.

"Why'd you come?" she asked.

I'd have thought that would be obvious. "To thank you."

"You could've, I don't know, sent a note."

"No choice about that, either. You saved my life."

She sighed. "I meant it when I said I didn't want you dead."

"I know." There was another reason I'd come beside gratitude. I needed to tell her something, and I didn't know whether she'd hear it from me. I held out a hand and hoped she would take it.

She didn't back away, but she didn't accept the touch. "I'm not coming out, Kevin."

"I'm not asking you to. I'm not asking you to forgive me."

"Good, because I'm not there yet."

"I'm asking you to listen."

She narrowed her eyes. "You have no power over me."

Not true, because she was fae now, but I would never use it. "Just listen."

She considered for a moment, then nodded.

"I want you to think about why you're in the water. What it means. What you want from your life. If you're all right with spending however many years mermaids live in this bayou, I'm nobody to tell you different. But if you want something more, I think you should go after it."

She glanced away, gaze pointed toward the setting sun. "You think you're the first person who's said that to me?"

"No," I said. "Who else? The whole group?"

She laughed at that. It sounded sad. "A couple of them tried to pull me out of the water. It didn't work out too well for them. Malek talked to me like you're doing. He's the only one."

"I'm surprised," I said.

"He set the spell that gave me the chance to become part of the water—because that was what I needed. It was my choice to transform. To make myself into something different. Something no longer human. He's an asshole and everything, but he's not an *asshole*, if you know what I mean."

I showed her a half-smile. "Yeah, I know exactly what you mean. He told you what I'm telling you now?"

"In so many words."

"You're thinking about it?"

She hesitated, but only for a second. "Yes."

"That's all I wanted to know."

"That's all?"

I nodded. "It's gonna get hairy around here. I don't know how soon. I might not be around very much to help."

She rolled her eyes. "Kevin, you don't live in this world anymore."

"Doesn't mean I can't visit."

"What's your point?"

"If you need anything, just ask. Okay?"

She met my gaze and held it. "Deal."

"And if you come out of the water, the rest of us could use your help."

"Okay."

Not much, but I'd take it.

I nodded and stood, brushing the grass from the seat of my pants. "See you, Amy."

"Bye, Kevin." She pushed away from the bank, treading the surface for a breath, then sank under the surface.

I turned away from the water and walked back to the lot. The crow in the oak took wing and circled above me, following me all the way. I caught sight of Rude through his windshield. He saw me at the same time, leaning over to push open the passenger door, flooding the night with a solid wall of electric guitar solo.

I slid into the Suburban, closing the door after myself. Rude turned down the tunes so we could hear ourselves talk. Hearing ourselves think was something else. I couldn't help cracking a full-on smile.

"It go okay?" he asked.

"Yeah. I have stops to make tonight."

"Figured," he said. "Your dad?"

I nodded. "I have no idea what I'm gonna say to him that won't freak him out."

"Don't even try, dude. On the other hand, he might be cool with knowing his kid is the new Faery King."

"He hates the fae."

"Faery. King," Rude said again. "He can quit worrying about the old King coming after him again and live his life."

I brushed the hair from my eyes. "You say."

"I do." He lifted the cigarette pack off his dash and tapped out a fresh one. "Where else?"

"Snake Bite," I said.

"Malek's." He flipped open his Zippo and lit the smoke. "Please tell me you're not getting inked there."

"I've already got new ink. Well, new to me anyway. It was Silver's, and now it's mine. I want to know the magic he put into it. Devil's in the details."

"You gonna tell me what happened to you?"

I laughed. "All about my summer vacation."

"All the highlights."

"Every single one. Even the ones you don't want to know."

"All ears, dude."

"We have all night before I have to get back." A whole night for me to be only human—or as close to it as I could get. I wanted to remember the feeling, savor it so I would never forget.

My father would yell before he paced and pulled at his hair and enumerated every single thing that could possibly go wrong. Then he'd relent and pack me a PB&J and watch me walk out the door with eyes filled with worry.

Malek would…who the hell knew what Malek would do? He'd give me the lore on my ink and tell me everything he could think of about Famine to make sure I knew what I needed to hold up my end of the magical brigade. He'd want to know what I thought about being half-human and half-fae. Or maybe I wasn't the first person that'd happened to, and he had lore to share about it that would make my life easier, or at least easier to negotiate.

I'd thought Malek was the Devil, once upon a time. I'd thought the same thing about the previous Faery King.

"You know, the Devil's not really in the details," Rude said, taking another drag of his smoke. "He's in the wind. We're gonna have to work together on this. Be ready when the next apocalypse hits the fan."

We'd saved the world, and I knew what for. We'd saved it for all the worlds. For the humans and fae and demons and angels who lived. We'd saved it to turn around and save it again. To keep saving it as long as we had breath in our lungs and strength in our hearts and hands.

One whole night to be human. Then down to business.

"Count on it," I said.

If you enjoyed this book, please consider leaving a review. It doesn't have to be long—even a few words will be very appreciated.

Reviews make it possible for an author to continue writing books in a series. They make a big difference in helping to get the word out about a book or a series. And reviews can make the all difference in the world when a reader wants to take a chance on a new author, but isn't sure whether they will like the book.

Thank you for taking hours out of your busy life to read. I hope this book brought you time to escape into a story, and that it brought you joy.

Turn the page to read the first chapter of **Angel Hunts**, Book 1 of the *Soul Forge* series, set in the same world as *The Faery Chronicles*.

LESLIE CLAIRE WALKER
AUTHOR OF THE FAERY CHRONICLES
THE AWAKENED MAGIC SAGA
ANGEL HUNTS
SOUL FORGE - BOOK ONE

# ANGEL HUNTS - CHAPTER 1

**P**ORTLAND, OREGON, stretched and yawned, awakening around me in the hour before dawn. I shivered as the November chill bit through the black fleece of my hoodie, and a wicked wind gusted from the west, spiraling the fine drops of mist in the air. The traffic light at the corner flipped from red to green, the hum of engines and the slick of tires on wet concrete a comfort to my wired nerves.

I stood beneath the dripping overhang in front of Justice Gym, go-cup of black coffee in hand. I listened and scanned the neighborhood for anything out of the ordinary. My life depended on it.

Twenty yards to the right, around the corner at the neighborhood stop-n-shop on Burnside, a car door slammed. Sleepy voices wafted my way. People stopping for smokes or snacks. Harmless.

To my left, the street curved and forked, parallel-parked cars huddled inches apart for warmth at the curbs. Out of the dark, the Orange Warrior materialized in his neon-orange rain suit, bike tires splashing through the puddled light of the street lamps. He caught sight of me and flashed the peace sign and called out, "Hey! Morning!"

I gave him a thumbs-up. Then he whizzed past on his way to work, the headlamp on the front of his helmet beaming like a search light, the red light on the back of his bike blinking fast enough to give somebody a seizure.

The golden halo around his body—the manifestation of the life force that moved through him—lit him up like a firework to my magical sight.

Across the street, the Stump Town Diner spoke the language of my belly, the rich aromas of dark-roasted coffee, salty, crisp bacon, and fresh-baked bread streaming from inside each time the door opened. Blond Bagel Girl, wrapped in her hooded purple raincoat, slipped inside for her usual breakfast to go. She shone with the same gold as the cyclist, though more muted, melancholy.

It was beautiful. Normal.

Normals in my neighborhood, going about their normal lives like clockwork. I'd never be one of them. I'd look over my shoulder until the day I died.

I turned the key in the lock of the gym door, same as every other day for the last three months since I'd moved to town. That my boss, Red Jennings, trusted a woman so secretive and new to the city with his life's work said a lot about him. A woman without much money and a teenage kid in tow, no less. Most people would call him a fool, but I chose to believe he was an uncommonly good judge of character. One who backed up his judgment with thorough background checks.

He hadn't batted an eye when I'd asked to be paid in cash, though; my existence kept off his books. When he asked the occasional personal question, I talked around it rather than answering directly, and he didn't give me any crap about it. He'd run a check on me and found it unremarkable. Of course, it was an unremarkable lie that I'd built through illegal channels and paid for with blood money, but all Red knew was that I wasn't a criminal, that he and I shared a home-town in Houston, Texas, and we shared a soft spot for troubled kids.

I pushed my way into the narrow front room of the gym, the electronic bell above the door chiming. I flipped the light switches with the flat of one hand and inhaled the perfume of rubber, bleach wipes, and sweat as the overhead fluorescents buzzed to life. The lights threw the entry into sharp relief: the interlocked, black rubber mats that covered the concrete floor, the triple-stacked row of black plastic cubbies and lockers that covered the long wall in front of me, and the donated, brown suede sofa on the right, its seats so deep I sometimes wondered whether it ate people as well as car keys and loose change. I keyed the code into the alarm, hung a right and then a left, bouncing down the short staircase onto the gym floor.

It shared the dimension of a good-sized basketball court. The walls had been painted white once upon a time, but had been scuffed and scratched to head-height. All the essential equipment hugged the walls: long barbells pegged into metal stands, kettlebells, weight racks, and benches for presses. Pull-up bars, medicine balls, wooden boxes for jumping. The back wall of the gym consisted of garage doors that could be opened in the summer for air flow. Two climbing ropes hung suspended from the ceiling. Also in back, a dozen rowing machines stood on end beside the water fountain, bathrooms, and small table that held the sound system.

It felt like home. First one I'd ever truly had. I had chosen it, and it had chosen me.

The first class started in thirty minutes, at 6:00 a.m. The usual suspects would file in: kids whose parents dropped them here before school trying to buy peace of mind—a little activity to help keep their progeny calm, quiet, and cooperative during a long day of sitting, obedience, and memorization. The usual suspects were anything but normal.

They didn't seem to belong anywhere, or to anyone except each other. They had halos that spoke of magic, all of it benign. They'd adopted my kid into their group as soon as they laid eyes on her, for which I felt profoundly grateful. Like Red had with me, they trusted her right away, even knowing nothing about her. For instance, the fact that she wasn't my daughter. She was no relation at all.

The first time I'd seen her, she'd been ten, close to the age I'd been when magic had marked me. I'd broken in to her house with orders to kill her family. To kill her. I hadn't been able to do it.

Faith Torres, her name had been then, before we'd gone into hiding with new identities, new lives, and nightmares that plagued our dreams. Ten years old then, now fifteen. Now she was Faith Sanchez, with dark chocolate hair that swung to the middle of her back, gangly arms and legs she hadn't quite grown into yet, and a hard-to-say-no-to million-watt smile. She also had a big, geeky love for badass super-heroines and a growing rebellious streak.

She'd sneaked out last night. First time ever, sometime between midnight and 2:00 a.m. When I'd made my nightly security round at 3:30, glass of tap water in hand, I found pillows under the down comforter and a window open just a crack, sucking in the cold. The water I'd downed on the way into the room flash-froze inside my belly at the sight.

I fought to shake ice-cold panic that told me the people we'd run from had located us and taken Faith, that there was no safe place and would never be, that the death I'd saved Faith from waited for her just around the corner, or maybe had already been dealt.

The Order of the Blood Moon's magical assassins were relentless. No one left the Order. They didn't forgive, and they didn't forget.

I shook off the panic. I calmed myself like the pro I'd been. Like the pro I still could be.

The Order had taken me in during a time I'd been desperate and vulnerable. They'd stripped me of my name, my identity, and the last shards of my childhood innocence. They helped me to marshal my magic, training me to gather information, conceal myself, kill, and elude capture. I'd given them my heart and soul because I'd had no one and nothing else to give it to. I'd allowed them to turn me into a stone cold killer. I'd done more than that—I'd embraced it. Our association had lasted fifteen years, until two months after my twenty-seventh birthday, the night I met Faith.

Looking at her empty bed, breathing through my fear, I let my training take over. I searched for a sign someone had taken her, but found no trace of foul play. After that, I'd pinged the GPS on her cell and located her at Ben's house. He was one of her new friends. His single father traveled on business too much and left him home alone.

Ben, who would never hurt Faith.

Still, I hadn't slept a wink the rest of the night. My girl hadn't climbed back through the window before time for me to head out for work—and I'd had no choice but to leave—so I'd put a note on her pillow. When she came home, she'd get the message and get her ass to the gym before school to explain herself. She'd show, too. No avoiding me, because that would be dumb. No one could ever accuse her of stupidity.

I made my way toward the back of the gym, setting down my go-cup on the shelf beside the sound system, then striking up my favorite classic rock playlist. I shrugged out of my hoodie and ran my fingers through my long, black hair, tying it up into a ponytail. I could fit in a warm-up and a few rope climbs myself while I waited for the door to open, getting myself in order before working the same movement with the kids. It'd take my mind off waiting for Faith as well.

The electronic bell over the front door chimed. I turned toward the whisper of denim and the squelch of wet shoes on rubber, expecting to find Faith walking in, a cranky apology on her lips and a sheepish expression on her face.

No.

Time slowed. I blinked, the movement seeming to take minutes rather than seconds. The air felt thick—almost too thick to breathe.

Before I even laid eyes on my visitor, the cadence of the walk struck me wrong, the footsteps belonging to someone heavier and with finer motor control of their body than my fifteen-year-old. I breathed in deep and tasted a hint of amber and vanilla in the air. None of the moms or stepmoms or girlfriends I'd met wore that scent. I'd studied each of them, remembered every quirky detail. I knew them. I couldn't afford not to.

I knew my visitor, too. I'd just never counted on seeing her again, because I'd never counted on seeing any of my colleagues from the Order again. Especially not this one.

The woman who'd walked through the door stopped ten feet from me, a signal she intended to talk rather than attack. Really, it was unnecessary. If she'd meant to harm me, I'd never have seen or heard her coming.

She pushed back the hood of her black rain slicker. Her blond curls had grown all the way to her shoulders since the last time I'd run my fingers through them. The only makeup she wore on her porcelain face was a pale pink flush of lipstick; her dark blue eyes were sharp on me. She unzipped her jacket, letting it fall open. A black brocade vest accented her long-sleeved black T-shirt. The ensemble hugged the curves of her breasts, skimming the line of her waist. Water soaked the hems of her black jeans. She wore steel-toe black boots with rubber soles.

Sunday Sloan. Once upon a time, my salvation.

The halo around her body held a tint of rose red, life force flavored with a strong, blinding passion that she harnessed in everything she did, including her kills. One look in the eyes of her victims, and she could literally blind them if she chose. She had a touch of the traditional psychic as well, not enough to actually see the future, but enough to guess what might happen that would affect her most and allow her to act accordingly.

The same magical gifts infiltrated her personal relationships. Her faults became hard to see. And once she made up her mind about a cause or a person, she gave them her unconditional, undying—blind—loyalty. I'd been on the receiving end of that loyalty. I'd thrown it away when I'd left without saying goodbye.

Sunday Sloan was the Order's MVP. Or MVO—most valuable operative.

If she was here, I was in deep trouble. I'd missed something important. Had I been wrong last night—had Sunday or someone who traveled with her taken Faith? Had they used their talents to make me believe Faith was safe at Ben's? Was Faith already dead?

How had Sunday found me? My passive magic—reading halos—couldn't be tracked by anyone. My active magic, on the other hand—using my power to influence others—could be. I'd been careful. I'd only used that active power on myself since I'd left the Order. It was the best way to unlock the secrets hidden in my own mind. And to stay sharp in case a day like this ever dawned.

I cleared my throat. "I didn't hide well enough?"

Sunday's voice had a liquid quality to it, like water flowing over river rocks. "You did. It's just that I know you better than the ones who're hunting you."

She'd just implied she wasn't hunting me, but that others were. If the Order had sent someone, Sunday would be it.

"I'm out, Night," she said. "Just like you."

She called me by my new alias rather than the name the Order had given me. It felt disorienting to hear it roll off her tongue.

"How did you get out?" I asked.

"I killed the Ghost," she said.

The Ghost. Brown hair, middling height, average weight. No distinguishing physical characteristics. He could pass you on the street and your eyes would skip over him. It wouldn't fool experienced bodyguards for more than a few minutes, but by the time they saw him, they'd be dead.

His mentor had named him appropriately.

He'd been our friend. One of the few people inside the Order I'd let in.

"He threaten you?" I asked.

"No," she said. "But he was in the way. He could tell something was off with me. He wouldn't let it go."

I closed my eyes for a second. A bit of my old life flashed forward from memory: lying in the fine, white sand of a Mexican beach with this woman before she'd been my lover, listening to the rhythm of the waves crashing, one after the other, on the shore, watching the cloudless blue sky with a clear conscience. The memory felt a thousand years old.

The Ghost had traveled with us on that trip, teasing us about our chemistry together. Sunday had killed him. She'd killed to get out of the Order. Or so she claimed.

"We were on the job in Lima," she said. "I waited until we took care of the target and phoned it in. We weren't supposed to be back at HQ for another week. I didn't think I'd get a better chance."

I studied her. The strong lines of her body, the softness of her face, and those eyes. I knew her tells. I saw none of them. Then again, she could've changed since the time we'd been close. She could've become an entirely different person. Looking at her now, I had to choose: act as if I believed her, or not.

She hadn't said a word yet about Faith. If she knew about me, how could she not know about Faith? She had to know.

"You want me to congratulate you on your newfound freedom?" I asked.

"I want you to say you're glad to see me," she said.

"Your coming here, making contact with me—you presence here blows my cover. If you still cared about me at all, you'd have stayed away."

"Night, the Order has no idea where you are. They don't know where I am. We're clear."

"I wish I could believe that," I said. "I've stayed alive this long by being more careful."

"Running and hiding," she said. "That's not living."

As if I didn't understand that. But running and hiding were all I had left. I had a responsibility to Faith, to keep her safe, to keep her alive. To make things possible for her that I'd never had. Would never have. Before Faith, I'd done what I had to do to stay alive. Survival had been my only concern. Now, Faith was my reason for living.

"Don't you want to know why?" Sunday asked.

"Why what?"

"Why everything," she said.

"I do." But only because it would help me to camouflage Faith and me better in yet another new city. God, I didn't want to leave Portland. Not when I'd finally felt as if I could stay somewhere.

"I couldn't live without you," Sunday said.

I raised a skeptical brow.

The corners of her mouth curved, but the smile didn't show in her eyes. "I wanted out of the Order because I was tired of the easy stuff. I wanted bigger challenges. I wanted to pick my own targets."

"That, I believe."

I understood that in the context and with the logic of my old self, my old life. My new ears listened to her words with dawning horror. She wanted to keep on killing. Not to stay alive or to have a place to belong, but for kicks. Or so she said.

She cocked her head. "Are we still friends?"

We'd shared every intimacy when we'd worked together. Now—if she told the truth—we shared a different kind of mortal danger. We'd been hunters, and now we were the hunted. And Sunday had embraced the monster inside of her. I felt cold all over.

"Why are you here?" I asked.

Heat filled her voice, rising with every syllable. "There's something magical rising in this town, something big and bad. I came to learn about it. To understand it. I came to fight it. I came to kill it."

I stared at her.

"I know you want in," she said. "We never got the chance to go up against a target like this one. It's the ultimate."

The ultimate? Whatever that meant. "No, thanks."

"The old you would've said yes in a heartbeat."

"I'm not her anymore."

My words seemed to sink in. She studied my face. "Just listen, then. Even if you won't fight with me, you should know what's here."

Faith and I wouldn't be here long enough for it to matter, but knowledge was always power. "Tell me."

"There's a Horseman of the Apocalypse in town," she said.

I blinked at her. "A what?"

"A Horseman. Like from Revelation."

I knew the Bible. My parents had been very religious. In fact, their religion had nearly killed me.

My magical knowledge base extended mostly to methods of intelligence gathering, concealment, killing, and escape. I'd come across other types of magic in my education and travels, but not as much about what Sunday suggested—that the Horsemen weren't fictional, and they weren't far-future creatures, but real in the here and now. "The apocalypse?"

Sunday nodded.

"*The* apocalypse."

She nodded again.

The actual end of the world. Not the ramblings of cult leaders who promised their followers deliverance but ended up delivering only death. Not the fervor of those who prayed for the end times in hopes of salvation, damn the torpedoes and damn the rest of humanity so long as their asses—excuse me, souls—were saved. The actual end, breathing down our necks.

"How do you know this?" I asked.

"The signs started about a year ago. At first, I thought my imagination had gone wild, lacing together clues from unrelated occurrences. But then six months ago, a city went dark. A big city."

"Which one?" I asked.

"I can't believe you didn't notice," she said. "Houston."

Not just a big city, but the fourth largest in the country. How could I have missed that, even busy trying to stay alive and under the radar? Because I avoided everything about the place. I couldn't remember the last thing—the worst thing—that had happened to me there. The very thought of trying brought on a razor-sharp terror that started at the base of my spine and clawed its way up into my heart.

"The city going dark—the magic that caused it—was it shielded?" I asked. "Someone wanted to keep outsiders from noticing?"

If it had been, then only someone with the magical ability to see it would've caught on. Everyone else would've skipped right over it for a few days as if a city that big disappearing from the proverbial radar was perfectly normal, not worth remarking on or even having a suspicious feeling about. And once the city came back online, they'd forget that for a time it might as well have not existed.

"Yeah, it was shielded," Sunday said. "The magic that shielded it was ancient, older than anything I've ever experienced. I got lucky, noticing."

There was no such thing as luck. With Sunday, it was talent, plain and simple. And she'd followed the signs here, to a Horseman.

"Which Horseman's in town?" I asked.

Her eyes twinkled. "I'm ninety-nine percent sure that it's Death."

*La Muerte?* "Jesus," I said, as much in reaction to Sunday's excitement as to the identity of the big bad.

"It's like fate," she said. "Or destiny. What we are—it's like we're related to him. We're his children."

I shook my head. "What you are, maybe. I told you, I'm not who I used to be anymore."

"It's impossible to wash that much blood off your hands, Night."

"At least I'm trying."

"You let me know how that works out," she said.

I had no intention of letting her catch up with me again. "Any idea what Death looks like so I'll know if I run into him?"

"He could look like anyone at all. Anyone."

"Great," I said.

"Your sarcasm is appreciated. You have no idea how much I've missed it." She crossed her heart with her index finger for emphasis. "He's Death, Night. He could be an old lady or a teenage boy for all I know—anyone who's been touched by death closely."

"So, what kind of magic are we talking about here? Shapeshifting? Possession?"

She shrugged. "Does it matter?"

"Technically, yes," I said. "If he's shapeshifting, then he's contained in his own body and can look like anyone he wants to. If he's possessing people, then he's a free agent, so to speak, and the people he's possessing could end up messed up at best and dead at worst. It matters because given all that, if you're looking to take him out, how will you even know it's him? And are you gonna be taking out an innocent person while you're at it?"

"The old you wouldn't have cared."

"Like I keep telling you."

She sighed. "I'm not sure one innocent life outweighs a dead Horseman of the Apocalypse."

"I'm sure the innocent and their family and friends would beg to differ."

"If you're so concerned," Sunday said, "then come with me. I wasn't kidding, Night. I need you on this."

I dodged the invitation. I'd said no once, and I wouldn't say it again. What I wanted now was more information, whatever Sunday could give me that would help Faith and me survive. "Can something that old and strong even be killed?"

"I don't know, but I have to try. Night, he's *Death*. Is there anyone else I could take out that would even come close? If anyone could do it, it's me."

I agreed. Sunday killed better than anyone I'd ever seen. I'd been good at it, but Sunday was out of my league. She had courage—and bravado—that captivated as much as the rest of her, an I-don't-care-whether-I-die attitude that drew me like a moth to the flame. I hadn't cared either, once upon a time. We'd been kindred spirits. Soulmates.

She'd killed a lot of people. It didn't matter whether the people she'd killed considered themselves evil or good. It only mattered that they were dead.

I knew that better than anyone else. Sunday could lecture me about the blood on my own hands all she wanted; I knew it would drip from my fingertips until the day I died and probably flood my grave. If there was a hell separate from the ones we created for ourselves and each other in this world, I'd be sent straight there, do not pass GO. It was where I belonged.

A fucking Horseman of the Apocalypse.

I knew from my time in the Order that there had been other apocalyptic close calls—the world had almost ended half a dozen times according to the Order's records. But none of those times had involved a Horseman.

If the end of the world was really nigh this time, taking Faith and running again might not work. If something happened to her, I'd never forgive myself. If something happened to me, what would happen to Faith?

"How do you intend to find Death?" I asked.

"You don't want to help me, I don't need to tell you." She dropped her gaze from my face to the scoop neck of my T-shirt, where the pendant she'd given me hung on its delicate silver chain. "You still have it."

The silver hourglass, a symbol of what I'd been and what I'd become. I had been death itself, and I had died to that life. Now, I had a second chance that I'd sworn never to waste. A new beginning. "I've never taken it off."

She met my gaze. "Even if you won't help me, do you really want me to stay away?"

I looked into her eyes, and at her mouth. I dreamed about the shape of her mouth sometimes, the way it celebrated all her moods. Part of me wanted to kiss her and taste the fire of the life inside her and the espresso I knew she'd have sipped on waking. Part of me wanted to drown in her, for things to be like they'd been before.

"It's probably better if you do," I said.

"C'mon, Night. Reconsider."

"Thanks, but no thanks," I said with more determination than I felt.

"I hear so much as a whisper about any of the Order in town," she said, "you'll be the first to know. Same if things get out of hand with the Horseman of Death."

"Thanks," I said again.

Faith and I would have to start the motions of getting the hell out of Dodge and be gone by day after tomorrow, tops. If I could get us gone by tomorrow morning, that wouldn't be soon enough for me. But my girl wasn't ten anymore. She didn't do what I told her just because I said so. She would need a reason. I didn't want to have to tell her that I'd somehow screwed up and our cover was blown here.

"Thanks for not killing me," Sunday said.

My lips twitched into a half-smile. "You, too."

She took a hesitant step toward me, then crossed the distance in a couple of quick strides. She wrapped her arms around me and hugged me tight. Her body felt familiar, like second skin. Her strength, the amber scent in her hair, the brush of her breasts against mine. She pulled back just enough to plant a kiss on my forehead, and then one full on my lips, soft and mesmerizing.

I tasted the espresso and felt the line of the scar that ran across her bottom lip, the one that lipstick camouflaged so well. My heartbeat quickened. My arms wanted to move of their own accord, to draw her closer. I did not.

She pulled away, a question in her eyes that she asked a moment later. "Did you meet someone else? New woman? New man?"

I shook my head. "No time for love."

How could I find anything real when I had to hide my past? When I had to hide my real name? Like Faith, I'd taken a new one—Night, because I'd gone dark, inside and out. Whoever I'd been before my parents had given me to the Order, whoever I'd become under the life-or-death training the Order had given me—that girl, that woman, were dead and buried.

I'd never be able to stop running.

Sunday studied my face. Whatever she read there, she kept to herself. "Take care, Night. I'm glad you're safe," she said.

She turned away and walked out of the gym, the electronic chime announcing her departure. My heart thumped hard in my chest as she turned left into the neighborhood, disappearing from view, as the last traces of her perfume faded.

I breathed deep, making my exhales longer than my inhales, slowing my heart and recalibrating my nervous system until I felt absolutely calm, until I could think more clearly. Sunday hadn't used her magic on me, but I still felt as if I'd been run over by a forest fire.

Ten minutes until I had charge of half-awake kids here to learn how strong they could be.

Faith should've shown by now. We should've already been through the show. Her apologizing, me telling her what she could or couldn't do, her throwing back in my face that I wasn't her mother and couldn't order her around. She'd had a mother, and just because the woman had died bloody and I'd taken Faith in didn't mean I owned her. I'd heard the speech a hundred times.

Thank God Faith hadn't walked in while Sunday was here. On the heels of that thought, another.

Armageddon: coming to my backyard. As much as I couldn't take a word Sunday said as gospel, who would lie about something like that?

I stared at the door, wondering who would walk in next. The Order? The Horseman of Death?

I didn't trust Sunday as far as I could throw her.

And where in the name of everything holy was Faith?

# ACKNOWLEDGMENTS

All my thanks and love to T. Thorn Coyle for helping to make this book the best it could be.

Wishing you stories, magic, and heart!

# ALSO BY LESLIE CLAIRE WALKER

**THE AWAKENED MAGIC SAGA**

THE SOUL FORGE

(The Complete Series)

Angel Hunts

Angel Rises

Angel Falls

Angel Strikes

Angel Roars

Angel Burns


THE FAERY CHRONICLES

(The Complete Series)

Faery Novice

Faery Prophet

Faery Sovereign


SHORT STORY COLLECTIONS

Ink & Blood

Ink & Stars

Ink & Sword

# ABOUT THE AUTHOR

Since the age of seven, Leslie Claire Walker has wanted to be Princess Leia—wise and brave and never afraid of a fight, no matter the odds.

Leslie hails from the concrete and steel canyons and lush bayous of southeast Texas—a long way from Alderaan. Now, she lives in the rain-drenched Pacific Northwest with a cast of spectacular characters, including cats, harps, fantastic pieces of art that may or may not be doorways to other realms, and too many fantasy novels to count.

She is the author of *The Faery Chronicles* and *Soul Forge* series, two complete series of urban fantasy novels, novellas, and stories filled with found family, angels, assassins, faeries, and demons.

*Connect with Leslie*
leslieclairewalker.com
leslie@leslieclairewalker.com

COPYRIGHT INFORMATION

**FAERY SOVEREIGN**
*Copyright © 2019 Leslie Claire Walker*
*Published 2019 by Secret Fire Press*
*Cover and Layout Copyright © 2019 by Secret Fire Press*
*Cover Design by Lou Harper*
*Cover Art Copyright © Lou Harper*



❀ Created with Vellum